DRE AMONG THE PAGES

RUCHA PANTOJI

Contents

ONE

"You look so beautiful."

My 5-year-old niece complimented me as she brushed my long curls until her arms couldn't keep up with them. She dropped the hairbrush and sat on my lap. "Now your turn. Do the braid hairband style," she demanded.

"Okay," I giggled and detangled her hair.

This morning, she woke up before me and declared both of us must wear matching clothes. I obeyed and wore my pink kurta to match her frock and followed her outside to the backyard where she could help me get ready.

We were sitting on the rug in the garden, soaking in the gentle morning sunshine. Birds flew from one tree to another, chirping blissfully. Purple periwinkle and shiny jasmine enveloped us in a delicate fragrance as September blossomed around us. And even though the rain would probably come and go till mid-October, the weather was clear and fresh.

For the past couple of months, rain drizzled almost every day. I enjoyed it for a few weeks until I started missing summer and desperately waiting for beautiful pink winter. Not that I hate rainy days. I do love soft sprinkles, but from the window, while I snuggle inside my blanket with warm tea and a good book. When I have to go out on those muddy roads, ruining my sandals and possibly the back of my jeans, rain doesn't feel that gorgeous.

I strongly believe that Bollywood creates a different illusion of monsoon. Love birds dancing under the rainfall, singing, laughing, and kissing. If I were the girl from the movie scene, I would first worry about my hair, then about my dress, and I would run straight home to take a hot shower before sliding under my blanket. Rainy days make me feel sleepy and lazy.

But today, the sun eased above the clouds and poured brightness on the entire city. Even my pets were in a good mood. Stevey, my 7-year-old Labrador, was rolling over the grass. Harvey the German Shepherd was happily pacing the entire lawn. Charlie the Beagle and Cookie, our 2-year-old Spitz, were playing with a ball. Everybody seemed pleased with the warmth spread across the backyard.

"Okay. All done." I brushed Nidhi's hair one more time and held up a small mirror in front of her face. She tilted her head from side to side and said, "I love it. Thank you, Avu Attu."

"You look like a doll." I planted a soft kiss on her head. A bright smile, with a front tooth missing, spread across her round chubby face.

Aai, my mother, was sitting next to us, watching our little make-up session. Nidhi turned to her and asked, "Ajji, do you want a new hairstyle?"

"You already helped me put my hair in a bun half an hour ago, Nidhi," Aai chuckled. Nidhi shrugged and fiddled inside my makeup pouch. She found a lip gloss and applied it to my lips. Then she looked at her Ajji again for permission.

"No!" Aai answered before Nidhi could ask the question.

She frowned and kept the lip gloss back in my pouch. "Ajji, you never let me do anything."

"You can do it when you are old enough," Aai replied.

"Have you forgotten I'm 5 now?" Nidhi grumpily furrowed her eyebrows.

"And that's not old enough." Aai folded her arms over her chest. "Ask your own mother," she teased.

"I will." Nidhi mimicked my mother by folding her arms over her chest and held her chin up. Her adorable angry face made both Aai and me laugh.

Moments later, Tanvi Vahini appeared from the doorway holding a tray of breakfast. She was wearing a sky blue salwar suit for the occasion with her hair tied in a braid. She smiled as she placed the tray on the rug and sat beside me.

Nidhi got up from my lap and showered compliments on her mother before asking, "Can I apply some lip gloss, Aai?"

"No!" Vahini shook her head.

"Why not?"

"Because it's time to eat. Let's do *Angat-Pangat*."

The moment Nidhi heard those words, her entire attention shifted from lip gloss to breakfast. She jumped in excitement. "Yaay!"

She loves it when we all sit in a circle to enjoy a happy meal together. It's the time when nobody is busy. We all talk and listen to Nidhi's school adventures. Sometimes she brings her mini kitchen set and pretends to cook as we eat. That's our Angat-Pangat. And truth be told, we enjoy it more than Nidhi does because she makes us forget all our worries.

Tanvi Vahini served Aloo Parathas on four plates and allowed Nidhi to serve the chutney on the side. We all enjoyed a delicious breakfast and Chai together in the garden, looking forward to the day to unroll at its own pace. I was glad that it wasn't raining on the day that I'd been looking forward to for years.

Today, I'm finally inaugurating my book cafe.

I spent years preparing for this day. And the past couple of months flew by with a snap of fingers as I renovated our bookstore into a book cafe.

My Baba created a paradise for bookworms in one of the row houses on Rhythm Lane almost 20 years ago. Harshad Dada, my elder brother, and I would spend hours in our bookstore after school, reading, trading books, and cherishing signed copies of our favorite authors. Once upon a time, it used to be a happy place where readers would come, chat, and buy books. The air used to be filled with the smell of new books and the happiness of readers. Everyone would discuss the fictional world more than the real one. It was almost like living in a dream.

But 4 years ago, our world stilled for a while. The bus Baba and Dada were traveling by to attend the literary event in Mumbai got crashed into a goods truck. It was all over the news. Out of 30 passengers, 8 couldn't survive and the remaining were severely injured. Unfortunately, Baba and Dada's name wasn't on the survivor's list.

The world around us collapsed like a castle of cards, turning our lives upside down forever. Losing two strong pillars of our family almost broke everything into pieces. *Almost!*

Before that phone call, I had everything. After that, nothing was the same. Not the house, not my life, not the bookstore that I thought would always bloom.

Aai did everything she could to hold our house together. Tanvi Vahini tried her best to smile for her daughter, but she lost her bubbly charm. And me? I kept picturing my future without my father and brother in it and I didn't like a single bit of it.

It took us a while to come to terms with our new reality. No matter how much we tried, we couldn't get a complete hold of our lives and the bookstore. There was so much to do. None of us had the heart or mind state to go through it. No matter how tight I held on to it, I felt like it was slipping through my hands. We couldn't deal with the idea of them not being in the bookstore. We did what we could. But I guess it was not enough. I thought the bookstore will work the way it always did. But of course, time changes everything. Nothing stays the same.

I couldn't see the store making only enough profit to survive one day at a time. And the only plan I ever had in my mind was to start a book cafe. I have always loved cooking as much as I love reading. It all made sense, to have my own café connected to our bookstore. I was 14 when I shared my dream of a Book Cafe with Baba. He was more excited about it than I was. In a life full of uncertainty, this was the only plan that I was a hundred percent certain about.

I realized I needed to buckle up and work thrice as hard to accomplish it. And until today, I thought I had more time to prepare myself. But time can never be enough, can it? The day I've been looking forward to for as long as I remember is finally here. *Without Baba and Dada by my side.*

My heart flipped a complete cartwheel of anxiety the way it always did an hour before my every damn exam. It's that feeling when you are prepared, but not confident enough to trust your guts. I could hear my heart pounding louder in my chest.

Calm down. It's gonna be okay. I told myself.

As we finished our breakfast and went back inside, Aai brought out a beautifully decorated Arti Thali from the kitchen. Her favorite purple saree and jasmine flowers in her perfectly curated hair bun, which now has a few strands of gray, made her look so beautiful. I have never seen her like this in a long time. She and Tanvi Vahini put a kumkum tilak on my forehead and sprinkled rice grains above my head as a Goodluck charm with the glow of Diya casting blessings on me. Nidhi, who was sitting next to me all happy, looked up at her Ajji with twinkly eyes.

"Yes yes. I can see you," Aai shook her head and sprinkled rice grains on Nidhi's head.

"Good Luck, Avni." Aai brushed her fingers on my cheek in a soothing motion. Her eyelids struggled to hold back tears.

I wrapped my arm around her shoulder. "Everything will be fine now, Aai." She blinked back a tear and ran her hand through my hair. I touched her and Vahini's feet and hugged them tightly. Nidhi snuggled closer to all of us and I pulled her into the embrace.

If it wasn't for my Aai's strength, we wouldn't have reached where we are today. It was Aai who stepped up and rowed the boat this far. In a life full of sorrow, Nidhi was our only ray of joy. Her baby giggles, her curious eyes, her first day of school, her first report card. It all kept us going. But the fact that Nidhi only got to spend a year with her father and grandfather, and would only have their blurry memories, broke our hearts. She had gotten used to their voices and cuddles. She noticed their sudden absence and would ask in her broken sentences why her Baba and Ajoba are not there anymore. None of us had answers to her questions. We never really talked about the level of our grief. Because some things are just hard to say out loud. And the human heart is a fragile thing. We have to protect each other's hearts.

In a life without Baba and Dada, our bookstore kept us occupied. But it's not the same anymore. It would never be the same without them. For now, I gotta work hard and maybe improvise a little to boost the profit margin that has been falling for the past couple of years. The only problem is, I have got no clue how am I going to do it. The thought of starting something new in hope of survival is churning my insides. What if I fail? What if the dream I showed to my mother and sister-in-law crumbles down? They've been looking forward to this change. I don't want to see them disappointed.

My Baba always said, 'Never entertain the thought of giving up. If one plan doesn't work, make another and another.'

Baba…Dada, if you are listening, I promise that the doors of our bookstore will never be closed, as long as I'm breathing. Today, "Among The Pages Book Cafe" will officially open.

TWO

"Hurry!" Nidhi chirped with excitement. "Let's go." Tanvi Vahini locked the door and we all began walking towards Rhythm Lane to our book cafe.

Rhythm Lane is just around the corner from my beautiful house. Here in Kothrud, one of the lively areas of Pune, things are both peaceful and chaotic. Traffic can be too much at times. But if you are lucky enough, you can spot a dancing peacock around the hills on rainy days. The place is a perfect blend of Maharashtrian culture and modern lifestyle. I haven't met a person who'd get bored in Kothrud.

Our little house once belonged to my grandfather. It's not massive, but big enough for us. It has a living room, kitchen, and one room on the ground floor and two rooms upstairs. Everything squeezed into a small plot. The lane is outlined with row houses from both sides, with a small backyard garden and a front patio. A walk from our house to the corner where Rhythm Lane begins is merely 10 minutes long.

With Nidhi's constant chitter-chatter, we all traced the path to our book café, closely accompanied by our pets. Stevey stayed closer to me as if to say *Don't worry hooman, I'm with you.* I patted his back to thank him. Harvey occasionally woofed at Cookie and Charlie who weren't walking in the straight line. But Cookie and Charlie continued their little morning adventure of jumping around.

We turned left from the corner and were greeted by the vibrant lane of shops and houses called Rhythm Lane. It indeed has a rhythm of joy.

I was only 4 when Baba decided to open a bookstore. He wanted a place big enough to fit loads of books and space for readers to sit and read. A rented shop would never have been enough. Eventually, Baba ended up buying a 1bhk house on Rhythm Lane where he could build the world of books. We used to order tons of books every month from various publishers, authors, and book distributors. And we also had my Baba's books on sale. Yes, my Baba was an author. Not just any author, the best-selling author Arun Joshi. His books on Indian history were once found in all bookstores. He even wrote historical fiction and sold thousands of copies. Many publishers were lining up to sign a deal with him. But after his death, all the books that he wrote faded somewhere. It breaks my heart. Baba could have done so much more. He loved writing as much as he loved his children. Now we have all of his books displayed on a shelf, and Aai tries to sell his stories as often as she can.

As we reached the store, the new calligraphic sign of *Among The Pages Book Cafe*' shone like sunshine. I walked to the door and brushed my fingers over the *Closed* sign. Turning it over to *Open* flooded my heart with immense hope. *This is it.*

I fished out the bunch of keys from my bag and unlocked the main door. It clicked and I felt a solid blend of anxiety and excitement. I pushed the door wide open to let my family in. When I walked across the room to open the backdoor, all my four dogs immediately bolted towards the garden. Leaning against the doorframe, I looked around myself. Fairy lights outlining the classic walnut-colored bookshelves twinkled with joy. Fictional figures complimented the books on shelves. The fragrance of books was dancing inside the café over the light breeze. Everything was exactly the way I wanted.

Last week, we reorganized bookshelves from the living room to make space for the café's seating arrangement. The majority of the bookshelves and bookcases are now in the bedroom, aka Reader's Corner which is big enough to hold a couch and a couple of armchairs. My personal criss-cross bookcase where I display my latest five favorite books now stands on the counter. This bookcase has been in the store for many years. Baba had come up with an idea for my own book recommendations, and I was over the moon to handle that little bookcase. I'm grateful that Baba decided to buy the entire house rather than a small store. Because nothing is big enough to store books. *Not even the entire world.*

I glanced through the front window that overlooks Rhythm Lane to see what my two best friends were up to. The apartment complex in front of our book cafe has 3 identical shops at the ground level facing the lane. The first one is a cake shop called '*Baking Magic*' owned by my dearest childhood friend Nupur. Her cakes and pastries are awesome, by the way. The shop next to it is a boutique, '*Rutu's Closet- Classy and Trendy'.* My second and fairly new best friend Rutu's shop. She sews, knits, and sells practically everything, especially party dresses and wedding lehengas.

The last shop, next to Rutu's, is where Mr. Chaturvedi, my Ajoba's best friend, has started a dairy with his wife. He is a retired school principal, from the same school where my Ajoba was vice principal, and the dairy is his way to stay active after retirement. The whole Rhythm Lane, from start to end, is outlined with various shops, co-working spaces, residential apartments, rowhouses, girls' hostels, and now a book café.

I wish Baba and Dada could see my newly designed book cafe. They would have been so happy. Remembering them, I made my way to the bookshelf and placed a new photo frame next to the stack of books. A picture of my family when Baba and Dada were still with us. It's a picture of happy times.

I took a final glance around, recalling the time when I started saving a small amount of money each month with my catering gigs. I spent nearly two years saving enough money to create a place with a homely vibe. Yet I didn't have enough to buy brand new furniture and kitchen equipment. So instead, I bought second-hand furniture that includes bean bags, armchairs, two sofa sets, tea tables, 2 sets of mini table chairs, a patio set, and an Indian Baithak, all purchased from flea markets or online. Vahini, Rutu, Nupur, and I arranged all the furniture last evening and it turned out to be interesting.

Satisfied with the decor, I glanced at the wall clock and realized that in about half an hour, our guests would arrive for the inauguration. I glanced through the window that overlooks the back garden to make sure my pets were okay and hurried into the kitchen to make Adrak Chai, Sandwiches, and Veg cutlets.

The bell over the front door twinkled, announcing the arrival of guests. I heard Nupur and Rutu mumble '*Beautiful Rangoli, Kaki'* to my mother and made their way inside.

"Avuu!" Nupur's voice screeched through the hallway and she emerged into the kitchen from behind the curtain. Her short brown hair bounced as she jumped in front of me, holding a box. Rutu entered right behind her, carrying a gift box of her own.

"What's this?" I asked excitedly.

"Open it," Nupur said, extending the box to me. I lifted the lid of the box to find my favorite red velvet cake. '*Among The Pages Book Café- Grand Opening*' was written on it with a little icing doodle of a book and a teapot.

"And this is from me," Rutu said, giving me the box wrapped in sparkly gift paper. I peeled away the gift paper and opened the box to find a stylish denim apron sewed by Rutu. My book café's name was embroidered on it with the same font that I use on the front sign. It was perfect.

"I love it," I said to both of my best friends. "Thank you so much."

"We're happy for you." Rutu pulled me into a hug. Nupur wrapped her arms around both of us and squeezed us tightly.

"Good luck," both of them smiled at me.

"Thank you. I hope things will change now," I murmured. Nupur and Rutu have seen me distressed about the bookstore. They've witnessed my entire family breaking down and standing back up to keep the bookstore open. Nothing is hidden from them.

Nupur gave me a comforting smile. "Everything will be fine."

I smiled and asked both of them, "Want a cup of tea?"

"Nah. I'll take it later with everyone. Tell me how can I help?" Rutu prompted.

"Me too," Nupur perked up. "We're here to help."

"Okay. Please check on my pets," I requested, slicing cucumbers. "God knows what they are up to."

Nupur laughed and tossed a slice of cucumber in her mouth. "On it," she said, making her way outside to fetch my pets. Rutu stayed to help me plate snacks and then went outside to help Tanvi Vahini.

By the time I arranged all the sandwiches on the tray, the cutlets on the pan were nicely crisped. I turned off the stove and plated everything with Chutney on the side. Moments later, a mesmerizing aroma of Adrak Chai blended into the air. *Perfect.* I poured it into the teapot and checked the time on my phone. The guest would be here any moment now. And soon enough, I heard Chaturvedi Ajoba and Ajji's cheerful voices.

"Avni *Beti*," Chaturvedi Ajoba called out. I quickly removed my apron and hung it on the hook on my way out to greet my grandfather's best friend and entire Rhythm Lane's Ajji-Ajoba.

"*Namaste*, Ajoba, Ajji," I smiled at them and bent to touch their feet. Both of them showered all sorts of generous blessings on me and handed me a box wrapped in navy blue sparkle paper.

"This is for you," Chaturvedi Ajji said. A soft smile melted across her pink wrinkly cheeks.

"Oh. Thank you, Ajji."

"Open it," Chaturvedi Ajoba eagerly said. I carefully removed all the tapes and unwrapped the gift paper. Inside was a box that I opened to find a matte light pink coffee mug. I took it out and found that there was a beautiful little doodle of a girl wearing a chef hat with a spatula in her left hand and a pan in another. *World's Best Chef* was written below the doodle.

I'd be lying if I say my eyes didn't fight back tears. It was the sweetest gift. Not because of the message written on it but because of the love it came filled with. I smiled at the 78-year-young couple who has been looking after my family like their own for years.

"I love it. Thank you so much, Ajoba."

"Mention not," he smiled at me. "I asked my grandson to order it online. Amazon?" He sought confirmation. I nodded.

"It arrived just in time," Chaturvedi Ajji grinned.

I placed the mug on the counter and gestured for them to take a seat. Soon, more guests started arriving. Mahima Kaki and Sudhir Kaka-Nupur's parents. Women from Aai's book club. Our local doctor- *Doctor Kaka* (who, by the way, has a real name but nobody calls him by that. He is Doctor Kaka of the entire lane). Our neighbors from the society and nearby store owners arrived carrying flower bouquets.

Nupur and Rutu tied a red ribbon to the door of the café. We called all the guests outside for the ribbon-cutting ceremony. Rutu handed her colorful scissors to my mother. Everybody standing behind us was excitedly waiting for the moment. Aai blinked back a tear threatening to fall and cut the ribbon to officially inaugurate '*Among The Pages Book Cafe*'.

Everyone cheered and clapped and woohooed. Our dogs woofed and jumped around me. Nidhi, who was in my arms, gave me a gigantic kiss on each cheek. It was the start of a new beginning.

After the ribbon-cutting, Vahini made sure all our guests were comfortably seated. Nupur and Rutu helped me serve Chai, snacks, and cake. Everybody praised my chai and asked for refills. I happily brewed some more fresh tea to fulfill the demand.

As the clock hit 10, everybody left to open their own stores, to get back to work, promising to return as often as they can. I cleared out the tables and wiped them clean.

My phone chimed several times on the table. I opened it to find 20 pictures of the inauguration ceremony from Rutu. I could see she edited those pictures before sending them to me. I selected a few and posted them on @amongthepages social media accounts, tagging @rutuscloset for picture credits. I quickly shot her a thank you message and was about to grab my diary to check today's agenda when the doorbell twinkled.

I turned around with a welcoming smile to greet the new guest. But to my disbelief, two people, who I or my family wouldn't expect to be here, stepped inside the cafe.

Madhav Kaka- Baba's cousin, and his wife Vidya Kaki were standing stiffly before me. I haven't seen Madhav Kaka and Vidya Kaki in a long time. Kaka never calls, never comes to meet us, and probably never mentions us. He used to visit our bookstore once in a while, mostly by the end of the month, and wouldn't talk much. I thought he was shy, but now I wonder if he was just not interested in having a friendly, warm family conversation.

After Baba and Dada's accident, Madhav Kaka made one point clear. *I won't be able to look after you all.* And with that, he left and never came back to the store or our lives. We never asked him to look after us. We could manage that just fine. But he wanted us to understand that we better not expect any financial support from him. We met at the family gathering, once or maybe twice, and spoke little to nothing. He basically is a stranger. Vidya Kaki is lovely though. She is a soft-spoken person, and I dare say, the opposite of her husband. I wish we had a better relationship.

As my so-called uncle and aunt made their way to the nearby sofa, I saw Aai and Tanvi Vahini rushing out of Reader's Corner to greet them. Vidya Kaki was wearing a simple yellow saree and her eyes were swollen with dark circles underneath them. I couldn't help but wonder what was wrong with her. She seemed sad and scared. Even though she was a couple of years younger than Aai, she looked old and tired.

When I regained my focus, I went to touch their feet, "Thank you for stopping by."

Vidya Kaki smiled at me and cupped my face in her palms. "You've grown so much, Avni. And how beautiful you are looking today."

I awkwardly smiled at her. "Thank you, Kaki." Next to her, my uncle was looking around the café. His eyes were critically scanning the place and I didn't like the look on his face. It made me anxious. I wanted to interrupt his train of thought or cover the surroundings so he wouldn't see anything. Instead, I asked, "What would you like to have? Tea? Coffee?"

Madhav Kaka turned to look at me and said, "Tea would be nice, Thanks," without any hint of love or smile. I didn't care.

I went to the kitchen to get some tea for everyone. Vahini and Aai sat with the guests to keep them company. I could hear them murmur something that I couldn't quite catch. I hope he wasn't here to show fake support because I wouldn't care.

When I went out with a tray, everyone stopped talking and stiffened uncomfortably in their seats. Nothing about them made me sit with them to have a conversation. I served the tea and excused myself into the garden to feed my pets.

As I was pouring snacks into each of their bowls, heavy footsteps echoed down the hallway, getting louder per second. I turned around to find uncle Madhav standing on the patio. I was planning to ignore his presence but Aai has taught me to be hospitable.

So I hesitantly walked towards him and managed to say, "Thanks again, for coming. It means a lot when a family shows such support."

He looked at me with a blank expression and kept his palm on my head. I expected blessings but what came out of his mouth startled me.

"Enjoy it while you can."

And with that, he went inside and moments later I heard the front door of the cafe shutting. His words sent a chill down my spine. I could feel goosebumps of fear on my neck. A strange force tied my stomach in a scary knot and my legs felt weak to move. What did he mean by that?

Thousands of questions flooded my mind until Aai came to fetch me.

"Avu? What did he say to you?" She looked worried. I wanted to tell her what he said but seeing her so scared made me decide otherwise. I didn't want to lie to her. But I can certainly keep things from her for the time being.

"Nothing much, he was looking around," I replied and went inside with Madhav Kaka's words constantly ringing in my ears.

Among The Pages Book Cafe

Where the real world meets the fictional world.

Chai

Amrutatulya Chai	20
Adrak Chai	20
Lemongrass Chai	20
Black Tea	15
Lemon Black Tea	20
Iced Tea(Lemon,Peach,Apple)	50

Coffee

Hot Coffee	30
Black Coffee	30
Cold Coffee	40
Cold Coffee with Ice-cream	50

Maggi Noodles

Plain Maggi	40
Masala Maggi	50
Cheese Umbrella Maggi	60
Masala Cheese Maggi	70

Burgers & Fries

Aloo Tikki Burger	60
Veggie Burger	65
Crunchy Paneer Burger	70
Egg Loaded Burger	75
Salted Fries	40
Peri Peri Fries	50
Cheese Loaded fries	60

Quick Bites

Crispy Veg Cutlets	50
Cheese Potato Pockets	50
Mini Samosas	50
Maggi Pakoras	50

Sandwiches

Corn and Cheese	40
Club Sandwich	50
Grilled Cheese	50
Bombay Masala	60
Paneer Sandwich	65
Scrambled Egg Cheese Sandwich	65
Double French Toast with Cheese	70

Pasta

(Penne/Spaghetti/Macaroni/Fusilli)
(Extras- Egg, Cheese 20 Rs)

Alfredo Sauce	120
Arrabbiata Sauce	120
Pink Sauce	120
Cilantro Pesto	140
Pasta Salad	130

Omelettes

Plain Omelette	50
Sunny Side Up	50
Masala Omelette	60
Cheesy Omelette	60
Scrambled Eggs	70
Spinach Mushroom Omelette	80

Rolls

(Extras- Cheese, Egg, Mayonnaise 20Rs)

Cheesy Potato Roll	60
Spicy Veggie Roll	60
Paneer Roll	70
Double Egg Roll	80
Chef Special Roll	100

THREE

My head kept spinning with a series of thoughts for hours after Madhav Kaka left. I've been feeling confused ever since. It's that feeling when you *have* something but not quite. Or you were feeling happy for a moment and suddenly your stomach dropped into a pit. My thoughts are hanging in between frustration and anxiety. And I don't even have the complete context of his words. What did he mean by 'enjoy it while you can?' What's going to happen later?

The more I thought about what he said, the more frightened I felt. I wish Baba was here. I miss him terribly. I know he is here, somewhere, among the pages of the books, brushing his fingers over the spine of hardcovers, reading his favorite books, writing notes for readers with his fountain pen. He would have loved the cafe. He would have praised me. And for Madhav Kaka's situation, he would have said, 'Don't draw any conclusions, Avu. Most of the time, we only know one side of the coin.'

What's the other side of the coin though? All I know is, what Madhav Kaka said didn't sound good. And I was really looking forward to this day. I spent years dreaming about wearing an apron and rocking the kitchen as people browsed the books. The thought of somebody, someone from my own family, ruining it never crossed my mind.

I tried to stop overthinking and do something productive. But my mind kept drifting away every time I tried to focus on my agenda. Eventually, I grabbed a cup of tea and picked up my current read. Sitting by the window on the sofa, I tried to push away all unsettling thoughts.

Reading kept me busy and distracted for a long time. The book was a page-turner. Too good to put down. I was consumed by the pages after pages of madness, and when I was snapped back into reality by the chiming of the doorbell, my heart prayed to see new customers. But...it was just Tanvi Vahini and Aai calling it a day to go home. Aai told me that she was taking Harvey, Charlie, and Cookie home with her. I hummed and focused back on the book to pass the time. Funny thing about the time is, when you are dissolved into the world of books, 15 minutes could seem like an hour, and an hour sometimes feels like a few minutes. I can never tell how long I've been reading until I glance around and make myself familiar with the real world again. I read until the second half of the book became thinner than the first half. And when I turned to look at the wall clock, the hour hand struck 8. If my calculations are correct, I was reading for more than an hour.

A soft fur lying around my ankles moved and I saw Stevey waking up from his nap. "Hey, Stevey." I ruffled his fur and scratched his neck. He yawned and shook his head to get a sense of the surroundings. I chuckled. "Me too buddy. We both lost track of time."

Outside, road lamps and shop lights shed a gentle glow on the path. Rutu's sewing machine was making a rhythmic noise. Nupur's cake shop was closed early today. I hardly saw them after this morning.

I picked up my phone and shot a quick message on our Whatsapp group.

Me: Anyone up for a cup of coffee?
Nupur: Yup!
Rutu: Count me in.
Me: Perfect. Putting the kettle on.

No matter how busy we all are, we always make time for coffee evenings. It's the time we really get to talk about things that otherwise could be confusing for eavesdroppers. We talk about random stuff. Most times it makes no sense, and that's the best part about these coffee conversations. It doesn't have to make sense.

I quickly brewed three mugs of strong hot coffee and waited for my two best friends to arrive. Nupur lives in the apartment building opposite my café with her parents. Her apartment is next to Chaturvedi Ajoba's, on the second floor. She arrived at Rhythm Lane when we both were 12. When her parents were unloading their luggage from the van, I waved at her from the bookstore and asked her to come in. She and I spent half an hour talking in our bookstore and haven't stopped talking ever since. A couple of years ago she started baking and selling cakes from her home and her business quickly blossomed. So her father encouraged her to rent the store downstairs to have her own cake shop.

Rutu, on the other hand, met us 2 years ago when she was checking out the shop to open her boutique. She stopped by my bookstore to enquire about the place and get to know Rhythm Lane. She looked extremely confident and stylish. I immediately liked her and volunteered to show her around. Nupur joined us and we all walked around Rhythm Lane, meeting people along the way. Finally, we arrived at our bookstore and had a coffee together. A week after that, Rutu set up her boutique and rented a room in the girl's hostel down the lane, to be closer to her shop.

Bonding over coffee became our thing and Rutu sort of became our elder sister looking after us with her bossy instructions. And now, we all spend our days running our stores and meeting for coffee whenever we can.

"Hiya!" Nupur waved as she entered the café, closely followed by Rutu. Stevey woofed a welcome as he heard familiar voices. The girls pampered him affectionately and slumped on the sofa, grabbing a pillow each on their laps. I handed them their coffee mugs and sat on the armchair next to them.

"So," Nupur asked, taking a sip of the coffee, "How was your day?"

"Honestly?" I sighed. "Not that great. But I'm sure it'll change."

"Yes!" Rutu reached out to squeeze my hand. "Things will work out. Don't you worry now."

I nodded with a smile.

"Something wrong?" Nupur asked. My smile probably didn't look genuine.

What can I tell them? Until yesterday, all I could think about was this book cafe. The decor, the menu, the kitchen setup, the food tasting, new shelf arrangement. And when I thought it will all change for good, someone ruined it with merely 5 words. Now I'm not sure what to do or what exactly is going to happen.

"Nothing's wrong," I eventually replied. "Just tired I guess."

Both of them knew I wasn't telling the entire truth, but none of them pushed the topic any further. Nupur leaned back on the sofa and said in a soft tone, "For what it's worth, we all have our dream shops running."

"Yup." Rutu raised her coffee mug, "Cheers to us badass businesswomen."

We clicked our mugs and laughed. Laughing felt so nice. Like it was stuck somewhere below all the stress and got a chance to slip out. Sitting in a book cafe with my best friends pushed all my worries away. I was smiling and laughing from my heart. Whenever we meet for a coffee, we end up cheering each other. Late evening coffee meetups are sacred in that way.

"Did you see what Chaturvedi Ajji and Ajoba gifted me?" I asked.

"We did," Nupur replied, chuckling between the words. "It's beautiful. He was telling everyone that his grandson can order anything from his phone."

"Yeah." Rutu laughed. "It was cute. He talks about his grandson quite often, but I have never seen him around?"

"That's because he rarely visits," I told her. "I think the last time I saw him was when we were both in school. We went to the scholarship exam together when we were 11. His name's Vihaan."

"Why doesn't he visit? Or his parents?" Rutu asked curiously.

"His father has to travel for the job. I don't know what exactly his father does, but they don't stay in one town for more than a year or two. That's what I have heard. Chaturvedi Ajoba says his son doesn't get many holidays, so instead, Ajji and Ajoba visit them in whichever city they are in."

Nupur tucked her legs beneath her and prompted, "We are neighbors. Yet I have seen him only once, briefly. He seemed shy."

"Oh hardly," I corrected, too quickly for my own good. "In fact, he was anything but shy."

Both my best friends sat straight and turned towards me to hear the story. "Tell us everything," Rutu insisted with a wicked smile.

"That scholarship exam we went to together? He called me dumb that day and made me cry," I began telling the childhood tale. "I was being friendly with him the whole time. But he was mean to me. Apparently, I had made two silly mathematics mistakes and marked the wrong answer. He found it hilarious and laughed. I wanted to punch him in the face but all I could do was cry."

Both my best friends looked at each other and then burst out laughing. "Sure. That's something," Nupur said.

"Well, yeah."

I had sobbed when Harshad Dada came to pick me and Vihaan up that day. 'I won't get good marks,' I had told Dada and he had smiled at me saying, "It doesn't matter Avu. This exam is not going to change how smart you are, okay? Now chin up, let's have ice cream." He took us to the ice cream stall and made sure I wasn't upset anymore. But 11-year-old me hated Vihaan Chaturvedi, the boy who made fun of me and made me cry. Because, as dramatic as it may sound, no man in my family had ever made me cry. Harshad Dada was the best brother in the world. He was a touch-my-sister-and-I'll-kill-you type of brother. I relied on him for so many things, including helping me with school projects. A single teardrop from my eyes and Baba and Dada would make it their mission to make me smile. I was a pretty spoiled daughter, you see.

"Anyway," I kept my coffee mug on the table, "What are you two up to?"

"Don't ask." Nupur rubbed her palm on her temple and sighed. "Rutu is being a giant pain in the ass."

"Hey! I just need a basic favor," Rutu replied in self-defense.

"What is it?" I asked, curiously glancing between the two.

Nupur shook her head and said, "Remember my cousin-sister used to live in the hostel nearby and we used to smuggle food for her through the balcony?"

"Um hm," I chuckled. "She would throw the pillow cover tied to a dupatta down from the balcony and we would stuff it with anything she wanted to eat."

"Don't give her all visuals," Nupur snapped. "I accidentally let that information slip and now she wants to do the same for her friend. She wants me to smuggle some cupcakes for her friend's birthday. Apparently, the hostel doesn't allow outside food."

"Really?" My eyes brightened up. "We should do it. I will come too."

"No!" Nupur looked at me with the deadliest look. "Are you mad? We are not doing that. If we get caught, it's bad marketing for my pretty little cake shop."

Rutu twisted her pink hair strand between her fingers and glared at Nupur, "I thought you were my friend."

"I can help you smuggle cakes," I offered, mostly to piss off Nupur. It's fun when she gets mad.

"Traitor!" She deeply exhaled and nodded in disbelief. "You two can do that then. I'm not coming. And buy cakes from someplace else."

Rutu and I both flashed a puppy smile at Nupur. "Pleaseeeeee!"

She folded her arms over her chest and rolled her eyes. "No," she declared.

"We won't get caught. I promise," Rutu said. "And it'll be fun. Please say yes."

Nupur looked turn by turn at both of us and sighed, "Alright, fine. But just this one time."

"Done." Rutu grinned at her. "Just one time." She winked at me and I fought back a giggle.

"We should get going now." Nupur hugged herself and pulled her sweater closer to her chest.

"Yes, I must go too." Rutu added. "My hostel caretaker lady gives me an evil look when I'm late. Not that I care, but I don't want to piss her off today."

"Give me a moment," I chuckled and walked into the kitchen to rinse our mugs.

Nupur held Stevey's leash as I locked the café and dropped the keys in my bag.

"See ya tomorrow." Rutu hugged both me and Nupur and hurried down the lane to her hostel. Nupur gave Stevey a peck on his forehead before jogging to her apartment. I turned around to trace my way home.

When Stevey and I reached home, I tucked him into his bed alongside Charlie and Harvey. I kissed them goodnight before heading up to my room. Sliding into Pajamas felt blissful. I climbed onto the bed and watched the sparkling moon shining in the dark blue sky. Putting on my alarm and keeping my phone face down on the bedside drawer, I grabbed a recent book that I have been reading. It's a murder mystery if you must know. And I am pretty sure I have identified the killer. 9 out of 10 times, it's the husband.

Two chapters down, my eyes started getting heavier and I struggled to scan the words on the paper. I tucked my bookmark between the pages, placed the book on the drawer top, turned off the lights, and closed my eyes, gladly embracing the sleep.

FOUR

"Come on." I tightened the lace on my shoes and pulled my hair into a tight ponytail. "Let's get you all to the park."

A week flew by at a decent pace since the day I inaugurated my café. I would say things are going well, but not as good as I had hoped for. I do need to plan so many things. But first, my lovely pets deserve a much-needed park visit.

Stevey, Harvey, and Charlie joined me outside, thrilled to go to the park. Cookie was asleep in Nidhi's bed, so I decided to leave her behind. Trust me, it's better that way. She is like that annoying toddler you think twice before taking to the mall. She is sweet but she is also accident-prone. So it's just us, four sane people if you count me.

We walked past the row houses aligned with ours and turned left to arrive at Rhythm Lane. Senior citizens and pet parents were enjoying the morning hour. The rest of the street was peacefully quiet. None of the shops were open except for Chaturvedi Ajoba's dairy. He opens it every day at 6 in the morning. I like his liveliness despite being the only person actually fully awake, as the coming customers are practically half-asleep. Chaturvedi Ajoba cheers people up with his smile and delightfully kind conversation. Everybody loves him.

"Good morning fellas," he called out to my dogs and tossed some biscuits for them to catch. "Hello Avni *Beti*," he beamed at me. "How are you this morning?"

I must say, his enthusiasm can put a youngster like me to shame. For a 78-year-old man, Chaturvedi Ajoba is pretty fit and cheery. I walked closer to his dairy while the pets enjoyed their biscuits. "I am good, Ajoba. How are you?"

"Oh. I'm good as usual. Extra happy today," he smiled ear to ear.

"And why is that?" I asked, following his gaze to the wall clock that displayed 6:45.

"My grandson is coming to stay with us," he replied, smiling through his eyes. "He has got a job here in Pune."

"That's great," I replied.

"You remember Vihaan, don't you?" He asked. "You met him when you were in school."

How can I forget the boy who made me cry? But after all these years, I doubt he looks the same.

"I remember," I replied awkwardly. "But it has been years."

"That's true dear," he said. "Well, he will be here by 10, as he says." Ajoba glanced at the clock again and added, "Wife is making his favorite Laddus and everything."

His happiness was reaching every inch of his face, putting a wide grin across his wrinkly cheeks. He adjusted the spectacles that rested on his nose and shifted his gaze to the milk packet he was sealing tight, ready to sell.

"Your dairy order is ready, Avni. I've also packed paneer, cheese, and butter cubes as you had asked for," he nodded at the bag carefully kept aside, containing my dairy order for the cafe. There was a sticky note on the paper bag with my name written on it in calligraphic Marathi.

I smiled. "Thank you, Ajoba. I'll collect it later."

When I was finalizing vendors for the café, Chaturvedi Ajoba was obviously my first choice for dairy products. He was so happy about it. He even introduced me to one of his friends who has a farm nearby for my vegetable order and stayed with me to finalize daily vegetable requirements. "She's like my granddaughter, give her a good deal won't you?" he had said to his friend who did give me a generous offer.

"No problem." He started sealing the next package of milk. Few local customers approached the dairy to buy milk, so I waved goodbye to him. "See you later, Ajoba."

My pets and I walked further down the lane to find Doctor Kaka with a broom in his hand, sweeping the floor of his clinic. "Good morning, Doctor Kaka," I waved at him.

He is in his 60s and unmarried. When anyone asks about his marriage, he tells a different story every time. Nobody knows why he is single for sure but he is happy and he makes all sorts of jokes about it.

"Good morning, Avni," he replied, turning towards me from the veranda of the clinic.

"Stop by anytime Doctor Kaka, for chai."

"Of course. Of course," he smiled. I waved him goodbye to let him get on with the day.

"Come on boys." We carried on through Rhythm Lane, passing by Rutu's hostel, to the end where the park flourished even greener in the monsoon. As soon as we reached the gate of the park, I unclipped the leashes and watched my dogs running into the park. They joyfully played over the fresh green lawn, occasionally woofing and nodding to other pets to say Good Morning. It's a small and well-maintained park with a perfectly mowed lawn outlined by colorful flowery plants. Swings and ladders for children to play and nice wooden benches for parents to sit.

There's also a tiny water pond where pets can drink fresh water every day.

My dogs love this place. And truth be told, I enjoy our park walks more than my furry pets. It's a fresh, peaceful, and happy place where nothing could ever go wrong.

We spent around 30 minutes in the park. My dogs played on the lawn as I walked around the jogging track, occasionally throwing frisbee towards playing pets. Saying goodbye to pet parents, all four of us headed back home.

Rhythm Lane, while walking back home, was rather bustling. As it was almost 7:20, the majority of the shops were open. Working people were rushing to catch the bus to work. Parents yanking their children to get on board the school bus. Laughter club senior citizens making their way home and some more pet parents emerging from various houses. It was happy chaos. A happening lane of people with busy lives. A nice sparkle to the peaceful morning hours. I inhaled the morning fragrance and let the surroundings soothe my veins. And with new energy and motivation for the day, we all traced the return path.

Once home, I took a nice warm shower and changed into jeans and a black T-shirt that said *Easily Distracted by Dogs, Food and Books*. Pairing it with matching stud earrings, I brushed my curls, letting them fall freely below my shoulders. My mirror reflection was a slightly relaxed version of myself. That is because I've decided not to overthink anything. Whatever Madhav Kaka said may not mean anything and even if it does, worrying won't solve problems. Instead, I will focus on the business as I had planned all along.

Last week, my friend from college called to tell me that her cousin-brother Amit was looking for a freelance gig. She said he can help me set up billing software. I'm always happy to pay locals, so I asked him to stop by the cafe today. The billing software and planning some social media posts are on my today's agenda. I grabbed my tote bag and left for the café, determined to check the to-do list

"Avu!" Aai called from the doorway. "What about breakfast?"

"I'll eat later, Aai. Don't worry," I yelled back over my shoulder and hurried along the path.

Before unlocking the book cafe, I quickly ran towards the dairy and collected my bag from Chaturvedi Ajoba. The fridge was pretty much stocked up for the day. I tightened my new denim apron and prepared all the necessary ingredients for the day in the kitchen, rinsed the cutlery, and was about to brew chai when the bell on the front door chimed. "Hello. Welcome," I walked out to greet the guests. Two young, professional-looking women walked in, carrying their work bags.

Both the women smiled back at me. "Hello. Good morning."

"Very good morning to you too. What would you like to have?" I waited as they scanned the menu card and whispered something in between themselves before saying, "We would like strong coffee and sunny side up, please."

"Sure," I replied. "Please make yourself comfortable."

The women preferred to sit outside on the wooden patio sofa set facing the garden, chatting about their work. I kept a fresh water bottle on their table and went into the kitchen to prepare their breakfast.

Once the coffee was nicely brewed, I plated the sunny side up with brown toast and sprinkled some salt and pepper on the eggs.

"Here." I served breakfast on the table between them. "Hope you enjoy it." Both ladies sipped coffee and closed their eyes to let the freshness dissolve into their bloodstreams. We chatted for a while. They told me about their work meeting and how they were nervous about it.

"I'm sure you both will do great. Good luck. And you know what? There's nothing a nice coffee can't fix." I beamed. "Another round? On the house."

"Really? That would be nice. You are such a delight, Avni."

We all had a round of coffee before the women rushed to work saying, "If we get the deal, we will bring our whole team to celebrate here."

That one statement made my day happier. I've been waiting for something like this. Things could get better, I just have to be patient.

After the women left, I spent some time reorganizing Avni's Book Recommendations. Each month, I change books on my recommendation bookcase on the counter. Mostly multi-genre. Sometimes, I repeat a book because it was too good. Today, the shelf has a self-help book on habits, an excellent book. A YA murder mystery, 2 romcoms (duh!), and one memoir of a female comedian.

Happy with my book arrangement, I made myself a sandwich. By the time I ate breakfast, it was already 10:30 in the morning. Amit said he would stop by before 11 to install billing software. So I sat by the counter and powered on the computer to check if everything was working fine. While doing so, I accidentally dropped the pen holder, scattering its content on the floor. *Damn it!*

As I was gathering the pen stand together, somebody entered the café. I looked up to see a man wearing black jeans and a grey polo t-shirt looking down at the mess. I quickly adjusted my posture to greet him. "Hi, Amit. I have already powered on the computer. How long would you need to install everything?" But Amit looked completely puzzled at me. His eyebrows furrowed at the center. His brown eyes scanned my face as if I said something completely random. "I'm sorry what?" he asked.

I found myself equally confused as him. It slowly dawned on me that he might not be Amit and I should have asked first.

"Are you...um...not Amit?" I awkwardly asked.

"I'm Vihaan," he replied. "Vihaan Chaturvedi. Don't you remember me Avni?"

My body stiffened with embarrassment and my cheeks flushed. After years, I met Vihaan for the first time, and I didn't even recognize him. I probably startled him and felt so stupid I could have just vanished right there. Aai always says, 'Avu you speak first and think later.' She is obviously right.

I stared at him, scanning his face to get a glimpse of the old Vihaan that I was familiar with. But the Vihaan standing before me didn't have a trace of the old Vihaan. This Vihaan has nice bouncy hair. His eyes, brown eyes, are deep and... I don't know... different. This Vihaan is tall and fit and rather- I can't believe I am thinking this- handsome. It was a weirdly pleasing sight.

I quickly pulled myself together to apologize. "Oh hey, Vihaan. I'm so sorry. Actually, I was expecting someone and assumed..." I paused and extended my hand with a cheery smile on my face. "Never mind, it's nice to see you again. Welcome to Rhythm Lane."

He shook my hand and looked around the place. "Interesting," he declared, taking a seat on the nearest armchair. "Ajoba and Ajji talk about you a lot."

I nodded with a smile, not knowing what to say next. I fiddled with my fingers as an uncomfortable silence lingered between us for a moment until Vihaan broke it.

"I also heard stories of your pets. Ajoba told me that Stevey spent an entire day at dairy during heavy rainfall to keep him company," he added, sounding pleased.

"Yes. My pets are quite fond of your grandparents as they always offer snacks."

A soft smile formed on his face. He picked up the menu card from the table and scanned the items.

"What would you like to have?" I asked, suddenly feeling flustered.

He looked up from the menu card and said, "Lemongrass chai would be nice."

"Sure," I started walking towards my kitchen, still gathering my thoughts around him. "Anything else?"

"No, just the tea," he replied, glancing around the bookshelves.

"Okay. Feel free to browse the books if you like."

As I brought Vihaan's Chai, Amit emerged from the front door.

"Avni?" He introduced himself, "I'm Amit."

"Oh, hi. Just a moment," I quickly served Vihaan's tea. "Enjoy the tea. Please call me if you need anything else." I kept a box of tissues on the tea table next to him and made sure he had everything in handy.

"Is that who you were expecting?" Vihaan asked, laughing.

"Yeah." I bit my tongue. "Sorry about that again."

"No worries." He took a sip of the tea and said, "Carry on."

I turned to greet Amit. He helped me install a billing system, a card machine, and a payment announcement machine and gave me a manual that had all the necessary information on it. I thanked him and paid him via e-wallet.

"Would you like a chai?" I asked him.

"No. I'm in hurry. Call me if you need anything else," he said before leaving.

When he left, I turned my attention back to Vihaan. He was quietly scanning the bookshelf with one hand in the pocket of his jeans and the other holding a teacup.

"Found anything you like?" I asked, walking towards him.

"I did." He pulled out a business book from the shelf and showed it to me. "This one matches my interest."

"Good to know," I replied. "I'll pack it for you."

"Very professional," he raised an eyebrow and met my eyes with his lips curled into a smile. His eyes had some kind of peace in them and his smile complimented his eyes really well.

I took the book from him and wrapped it in a paper bag. "Here," I extended the bag to him. "Happy Reading."

"Thanks." He looked straight at me with, if I'm not mistaken, a slight curiosity. I tried to study his face, wondering what he might be thinking. I don't know why I wanted to know what was going on in his mind.

When he raised an eyebrow at me, I realized that I was staring at him for too long. Blinking quickly, I managed to straighten up my mind to start a different stream of conversation.

"So," I opened the Book database on the computer to update the number of copies of the book Vihaan purchased, just to avoid eye contact. "Heard you got a new job here?"

"Yes," he replied, hovering near the counter as I rang up his order. "Starting from tomorrow."

"What do you do?" I asked out of the blue.

He ran fingers through his hair and answered, "I'm a software developer. I did freelance for a couple of years and now got a job here."

I printed his bill and handed it over to him. "That's great. All the best. And welcome back to Pune."

"Thanks," he smiled at me. "I'll stop by again tomorrow. Probably with Ajji and Ajoba. In fact, they sent me here to see 'what Avni has done to the bookstore'. And I must say, it's really nice."

I felt the lobes of my ears turning into all shades of scarlet. "Thank you," I mumbled.

He twisted the handle of the paper bag in his hand and said, "You were always smart."

Something inside me bubbled up as I heard those words. I opened my mouth to reply but waited to find the right words.

"What?" he asked, confused by my reaction.

I cleared my throat and narrowed my eyes at him. "I remembered something that contradicts your last statement."

"Oh?"

Of course, he had forgotten all about it. I mean, it's not something to remember or care about, really, but 11-year-old Avni was hurt. I had to defend her.

"Don't you remember calling me dumb and making me cry after the scholarship exam? The mathematics mistake?"

"Oh." He laughed. "I had forgotten about that."

"Of course," I said, rather dryly.

"You can't possibly be still upset about that?" he said, still chuckling. "We were kids."

"Um hm," I nodded.

He looked all over my face, clearly failing to read my expressions, and laughed again, "Those really were silly mistakes though."

"You have got to be kidding me." I burst with anger.

"What?" he said. "These are the things you laugh about in your adulthood."

"I just remembered." I folded my arms over my chest.

"What?"

"That I don't like you. In fact, I hate you."

"Hate is a strong word, Avni. Are you sure about that?" His lips curved up again and it suddenly became difficult for me to focus, or stay mad at him.

But now it was on.

"I'm pretty vengeful," I held my chin up and continued, "With deadly weapons in my kitchen and books on how to hide dead bodies on my shelf."

He held his hands in the air. "Wow. I don't want to become enemies with," he rubbed his thumb on his chin, "cry-babies? Is that the correct word?"

My insides started burning. I could feel flames coming out of my ears. "What did you just call me?"

"Didn't you cry after that exam for silly reasons?"

"Run," I gritted my teeth. "Run for your life, Vihaan Chaturvedi."

He laughed right from his heart and something inside me melted into a puddle. So sudden. So new. Unfamiliar with the feelings popping up in my heart, I tried to contain myself.

"I don't like you." I stayed firm, trying to keep my wobbly legs steady on the ground.

He looked into my eyes and said without blinking, "I'm sure we can change that."

Before I could say anything, he walked outside, leaving me confused and mad at the same time.

FIVE

The best part about my room is, I have two large windows aligned east-west. It gives me glimpses of all the different shades of the sky at sunrise and sunset. And it's beautiful to be accompanied by twinkling stars and the moon at the night. Feels like they are looking after me.

I was settled on my bed, shuffling pictures on my phone that I clicked last week. Pictures of books, teapots and cups, Nidhi reading a book and eating a sandwich, and my pets playing in the garden. Handpicking a few good ones, I scheduled those pictures on 'Among The Pages' social media for the next morning.

I was planning to read a book on my phone's Kindle app but got distracted by social media. Bookstagram has some great ideas to share pictures of books that I want to recreate. I am planning to display books under different trope categories in the cafe, just for fun. Enemies-to-lovers. Grumpy-Sunshine. Badass-female-characters. I scrolled through my Instagram feed, which is a combination of books and food. It gives my mind some peace when I see books and food on my screen. The world still has plenty of things to be happy about.

As I scrolled through #kindleunlimitedbooks, I came across the same business book that Vihaan bought this morning. That made me wonder whether Vihaan has an

Instagram account. Everyone's on Insta these days, instead of Facebook. Facebook is officially taken over by people who understand nothing about hashtags or the fact that it's just social media and you are not supposed to take it seriously.

I typed his name on the search bar and a couple of Vihaan Chaturvedi profiles popped up. I clicked on the one that looked familiar.

His profile was open so I could see his bio and pictures. *I build software applications. Sports|Marvel|Occasional Gamer.* Who writes a social media bio like a resume? Seems more like a LinkedIn bio than Instagram.

He has posted only 6 pictures with short captions. If anyone decides to stalk him on social media, they won't find much about him. Such a private person. Not that I share everything on Instagram. My personal account is private, but I write long captions. If my profile wasn't private, anyone would know what I do, where I live, and what would be the right time to kidnap me. Okay, that's a bit much. But hey, I read books. My head is full of scenarios.

I considered following him on Instagram, but that would seem desperate. I'd wait till he sends me the *Follow Request*, so that I can accept it with dignity. I glanced at the time on the top corner of the phone only to realize I spent half an hour on Instagram. Instantly regretting it, I kept my phone aside and rolled on my back. A distant buzz of vehicles and the soft rustle of leaves seemed to work like a lullaby. I was dozing off in the comfort of the night when my phone made a sudden screeching noise. I assumed it would be either Nupur or Rutu with some middle-of-the-night crisis, but the message was from an unknown number.

'Is this Avni?' The message read. I usually don't reply to unknown numbers. But this person knew my name and I thought it could be about my book cafe. I hesitated before typing back- 'Yes! Who is this?'

Instead of answering my question, the person, whoever it was, sent a couple of pictures. I downloaded them to find two documents dated 20 years ago when the bookstore was opened. First, I thought this could be a mistake. But the documents had Baba's and Madhav Kaka's names and signatures. What the hell was this? What Madhav Kaka has to do with the store?

Bracing myself, I read through the documents. It had all the legal information about the bookstore. Now I was wide awake. I zoomed in on the image and tried to read it very carefully. Madhav Kaka was...*is* the owner of 25% of the store and monthly profit. When I read all the clauses of the contract, a particular clause pierced the center of my heart- Any changes to the business structure can only be done if all owners have a unanimous agreement.

My heart skipped a beat. Why would my Baba involve Madhav Kaka in our business? Why did I not know about this? And what does that clause mean for my café?

I felt tears rolling down my cheeks. This can't be happening. I have to ask Aai about it. She must know something. We didn't get the chance to talk about Madhav Kaka's questionable visit yet. There's something that I'm not aware of and I have to know it. I can't just let anyone take over my Baba and Dada's hard work.

My fingers abandoned the grip on the phone and it slid down my palm. I let it fall free on the mattress and slumped back on the bed. Outside, the wind got a little aggressive. Tree leaves started making unpleasant noises. It was going to rain, definitely, and I found it distressing. Or was I imagining it? Either way, I couldn't fall asleep after that. I just closed my eyes, put on my earphones, and played the audiobook for hours, until the crack of dawn.

I stayed in bed for a long time, still wondering what would happen to Among The Pages. My eyes were burning and I couldn't move. After some time, my usual alarm went off but I didn't feel like doing anything.

"Avu Attu!" Nidhi's sweet little voice traveled from her room to mine. I heard her tiny legs thumping on the ground as she entered my room. She climbed on my bed with a soft toy dangling by her arm.

I opened my arms and let her snuggle in with me. She buried her face under my neck and murmured, "I don't want to go to school today."

I pulled her closer to me and whispered in her ears, "Should we tell your teacher your tummy hurts?"

She giggled and my god that's the most beautiful sound in the whole world. "Can we do that?"

"I don't think so," I said. "Why do you want to skip school?"

"It's raining out there," she replied. "I want to sleep more."

I laughed and planted a soft kiss on her forehead. "How about I help you get ready and drop you at school?"

She immediately sat up on the bed and flashed me a toothless smile. "Yes. You and I go together."

I smiled. "Okay."

She hugged me and held my hand in her tiny palm, "Come on then, let's get ready together."

And we did. I washed her hair, dried them, and tied them into two ponytails. She brushed my hair in exchange and helped me select an outfit for the day. Once we were ready, she asked Tanvi Vahini to click a picture of both of us and demanded to set it as wallpaper on my and Vahini's phone. "Now we have the same wallpaper. Don't change it, okay?"

She warned me.

"I wouldn't," I promised and kissed her soft chubby cheeks. Both of us had our breakfast and walked to her school under the umbrella. On the way, she kept talking in her sweet voice and made me feel so special about being her aunt. I couldn't have asked for anything else at that moment.

When I dropped her at the school gate and bent down to kiss her, she wrapped her arms around my neck and hugged me so tightly, if the school bell hadn't rung, I wouldn't have let her go. But she had to go. I blew a kiss at her which she caught in her tiny palm and waved at me until she was inside the classroom.

I will do anything to make her happy and feel safe. She deserves everything great in this world. Whatever Harsh Dada would have done for her, *I* will do it for her. *I promise, Dada.*

I walked back to Rhythm Lane, making a mental note of talking to Aai about Madhav Kaka. A quick search on the caller ID app told me it was Madhav Kaka's number last night. I haven't yet decided if I should tell her about the documents I received from him. It would freak her out. I can handle it all alone. I just need to know the whole thing.

When I reached the book cafe, Aai and Vahini were already there. Seeing them arrange books in the Reader's Corner filled my heart with warmth. I want them to have this, the place where they feel cozy and read their favorite books remembering their husbands.

I dropped my bag behind the counter and made my way to the kitchen to put on some tea to brew. Keeping everything prepared for the day, I poured tea into three cups and greeted my mother and sister-in-law in the Reader's Corner.

"Oh. About time," Vahini said, taking the cup from the tray. "Smells so nice. Thanks, Avu."

I smiled at her and waited for Aai to finish the task at hand. "Do you have a moment, Aai?"

"For you? Let me think."

Tanvi Vahini giggled and Aai laughed at her own humor.

"Very funny," I rolled my eyes.

"Come," Aai patted on the rug, next to where she was sitting among the books, "Sit here with us."

I sat cross-legged next to her. We had tea together and I waited for them to enjoy it before bringing up the topic.

"Aai?" I cautiously asked, "Why were Madhav Kaka and Vidya Kaki *really* here?"

Aai's expressions suddenly shifted. She exchanged a concerned look with Vahini and avoided my gaze.

"What is it?" I asked impatiently. Her reaction was making me more anxious to know the truth.

"There's a lot to tell, Avni," Aai sighed.

"I want to know it all," I replied softly, resting my hand on her arm.

Aai drew a deep breath, kept her teacup to the side, and began talking, "When Arun decided to start a bookstore, he was slightly low on funds. He had all these big plans, to create a bookstore where readers and writers can come together to enjoy the literary world. He couldn't just put all of his savings into it, so he decided to take a loan."

I braced myself. Financial conversations make me uncomfortable. Money can either build people or ruin them forever. One wrong shift and it all goes down the rabbit hole where nothing is wonderful.

Aai continued, "Loan was taking too long to process and this house he wanted to buy on Rhythm Lane for the store was up for a sale. He didn't want to wait for the loan. Your

Ajoba wanted to invest some of his savings into the bookstore without anything in return. Of course, Arun wasn't planning to just take the money, so he decided to offer a share of the store in exchange. Ajoba kept saying, *families don't do business deals like these*, but your Baba was a man of principles."

"Then what happened?" I asked, curious but terrified at the same time.

"That money wasn't sufficient. Buying this place, furnishing it, getting the inventory sorted, there was a lot to do. Arun didn't want to financially burden your Ajoba. At that time, Madhav Bhau said he is interested to be a part of the store. He said he'll not only invest money but also work with Arun at this bookstore. Madhav Bhau wanted to make it 50-50."

"What did Baba say then?" I asked.

"Arun only offered 25% to Madhav Bhau. And they made some sort of conditional agreement. Arun didn't want to be in favor of Madhav Bhau, so he made sure everything was suitable for both of them.

Your Ajoba was not happy about it, he kept saying he'll invest money without any partnership. But your Baba said, *Madhav wants to help, be a part of it. It's okay.*"

I could imagine my Baba saying those exact words. He was too kind and good for this world. He never saw anyone's bad side or never judged anyone. He should have, though, this is his hard work.

"A few years later," Aai continued further, "Arun decided to Add me, Harshad and you as business successors. He asked Madhav Bhau if he would like to add Vidya's name as they don't have any children. But Madhav Bhau declined and created a fuss about adding successors so early. Arun just wanted to make sure that if something happened to him, we will have legal rights on the store to avoid conflicts with Madhav Bhau. After that day, Madhav Bhau stopped coming to the store. He would only arrive once in a while to claim his monthly profit split until, eventually, he completely stopped visiting. Arun always sent him the profit cheque, though."

Aai dabbed the corner of her saree on her forehead and sipped some water. I let the information sink in. After a long silence, I managed to ask, "So what did he say the other day?"

"He said," Vahini's face was full of concern, "that he is still the partial owner of the store and you can't just make these big changes without consulting his opinion. You have to ask him, let him make decisions."

"And?"

"I said, it's not like we are doing anything illegal. We have all the paperwork. To which he said, he wants his invested money back. And if we don't have that much money, I think he might take over the store until we pay him back."

Those words shot a pang of fear down my spine. But I didn't want to surrender to that feeling. I thought for a moment, and asked, "Why now though? After all these years, why now?"

"I don't know," Vahini replied. "And the thing is...," she looked at Aai to seek permission and Aai nodded her approval. "He has given us two months to pay him back otherwise we don't know what he'll do."

I shuddered. A strong wave of anxiety and fear went humming down my veins. Two months? That's not enough at all to arrange such a big amount of money. I wanted to scream. I wanted to ask more questions but I was afraid to know the answers. I wanted to tell them about the documents I received. But they'll freak out.

I knew I needed to think this through without panicking. I took a couple of deep breaths to calm my nerves. My family was worried and I had to do something, say something. So I did, whatever came to my mind.

"You two don't need to worry. I'm sure we can do something. I will see if we can get a business loan, or I'll take more catering gigs. I don't think there's anything we need to worry about right now. It's just the money, we can arrange it."

"I have a couple of Fixed Deposits," Aai added.

"Me too. And some of my jewelry. I don't even wear it anymore."

My heart shattered into a million pieces when I heard those two sentences. Is this how it's going to end? Emptying my Baba's hard work, Vahini's beloved wedding jewelry that Harshad Dada gave her, which someday would belong to Nidhi. I can't believe the reason for my family's distress is my own family member. Family is supposed to be there to get you through thick and thin, safely. Not supposed to become the reason for your stress and illness. But I guess that's the story of every household. People take their loved ones for granted and crush their feelings like it doesn't matter at all. It matters though. It matters more than a million dollars.

SIX

"You know, when I was your age, I used to play in the playground with my friends for the entire evening," Doctor Kaka said to an extremely busy Nidhi. She finished her homework early and demanded to watch cartoons on Vahini's phone. We all know very well that if she gets the phone, she won't let it go for hours. So, Vahini asked Doctor Kaka to tell Nidhi a story until she and Aai finished their evening book club in the garden.

Nidhi turned her attention from the phone screen to Doctor Kaka, almost annoyed by his constant distraction, and asked, "Are you a hundred years old now?"

He looked at her with eyes as wide as a saucer and struggled to come up with a reply. I chuckled at my niece's abruptness.

"Do I look like hundred years old to you?" Doctor kaka asked.

"I don't know," Nidhi confessed. "You have white hair and a white mustache. You must be really old."

He rolled his eyes, "Yeah. I don't need reminding. And I'm as young by heart as you are."

"Really?" She grinned and said, "Then would you play badminton with me?"

"Do you know how to play it?"

"You can teach me," Nidhi added quickly before he could change his mind.

Doctor Kaka did not see that coming. He turned to look at me for help but I shrugged. He sighed deeply and got up from the seat cupping his knees in his palms. He held Nidhi's tiny hand and turn towards me, "Tell Tanvi she owes me 1 free book."

I giggled. "Will do."

Nidhi and doctor Kaka made their way to the park to play badminton.

"Bye Avu Attu," Nidhi called out before leaving.

"Bye bye!" I waved at my adorable little niece and sat down behind the counter to do some budgeting. I have to figure out how am I gonna pay back Madhav Kaka sooner. The numbers weren't quite promising, to be honest. The amount is big, certainly not something I can arrange in 2 months. It'll empty all our savings and emergency fund.

Resuming my catering gigs is one of the options. It still won't be enough, but it will be something. Some of my old clients still contact me to ask if I can take the catering contract. I can send them follow-up messages. Any lead would be good enough for now.

I buried my face in my palms to take a moment to myself. The bell over the door jingled as 3 boys and 3 girls with their backpacks dangling from their shoulders entered the cafe. Probably students from the nearby engineering college.

"Hi! welcome," I greeted them and waited for them to settle on the bean bags. They all opened their laptops, sprayed stacks of papers, notebooks, and pens on the table, and scanned the menu card.

"Hi!" One of the girls turned to reply. Her cheerful smile lightened up her eyes. She looked smart in those cat-eyed pair of glasses and denim jacket.

"Ready to order?" I smiled at the group and noted down their massive order in my notepad. "Anything else?"

"That'd be all. Thank You," replied the girl.

"Okay, please be comfortable. I'll be right back."

In the kitchen, I could hear them murmur about their assignments, complaining about their annoying professors who couldn't push the deadline for a single day. "...I mean, it's not like we were asking for a week. Just a day," one of the girls said.

Smiling to myself, I remembered my college friends and that wonderful phase of my life. College days are magical. It's the age when you are not a kid anymore but also not adult enough to have a sense of responsibility. You believe in yourself and have big dreams and wings that can expand to the sky. Watching these students, I wished I could go back to that life.

But at the moment, I needed to prepare 6 glasses of cold coffee and plenty of things. *Okay Avni, let's get started.*

Keeping all ingredients and utensils in handy, I first started with the pasta, both penne, and spaghetti. As pasta was already boiled and the sauces were pretty much ready, I just had to put everything together.

I sprinkled a teaspoon of oil in the pan and added onion-garlic and vegetables. A perfect sizzling sound irrupted from the pan. Sautéing it with the spatula, I let the vegetables catch the crunch before adding the sauce and the seasoning. With my favorite pair of tongs, I mixed the pasta with the sauce. Sprinkling some cheese, chili flakes, and oregano on it, the plating was done. Assembling a sandwich has become a part of my life now, I do it so quickly that you'd be surprised to see my hands working like a Porsche.

Standing in front of the gas stove that once belonged to my Ajji, I recalled how she taught me to be organized in the kitchen. *It's not just what you present, it's also about what you leave behind, which is a spotless kitchen.* She trained me to become, what we call in the Marathi language, a *Sugaran*, a kitchen queen. She would say, *remember, the way to someone's heart goes from their stomach,* which I believe is very accurate.

I wiped the countertop and the gas stove before plating sandwiches. Outlining six glasses with chocolate syrup from the inside, I poured cold coffee topped with cocoa powder.

When I went out, students were busy discussing their project. I carefully placed the tray on the table, ensuring no harm to their laptops or notebooks.

The girl smiled at me and said, "Thanks Avni Di, we're starving."

I blinked with a pleasant shock. "You know my name?"

"Yes," she said. "Vihaan Dada told me."

"How do you know him?" I asked, unnecessarily louder.

"Vihaan Dada recently joined a company where my brother, Nishant Dada, works. They have become good friends. He told me about your book café when he visited our house yesterday. So we thought why not have group studies here," she smiled, looking around in the café. "And I love books. So I instantly loved the place when I checked your cafe's Instagram page."

My heart lightened up. "What's your name?" I asked.

She adjusted her spectacles and chirped, "I'm Prachiti. Nice to meet you."

"Nice to meet you too, Prachiti. I am really happy to have you here. Feel free to browse books whenever you take a break."

"Thanks, Avni Di," she replied and shifted her focus on her laptop.

I left them to do their homework and made my way to the kitchen. As I walked past the front window, I saw Vihaan on the balcony of Chaturvedi Ajoba's apartment, working on his laptop. His hair was wet and looked ridiculously good on him. I watched as he ran fingers through his hair, adjusting them away from his forehead. But his attempt wasn't very successful as his hair fell back on his forehead like there was no better place for them to be. And I felt an unfamiliar type of jolt in my heart and a sudden urge to brush my fingers through his hair. *That's enough, Avni.*

I cleared my mind and was about to walk away when he shifted in his chair and spotted me looking at him. I wanted to thank him for recommending my café to his friends. But it took every ounce of my calmness to not fly to his balcony and break his nose because as soon as he spotted me, he rolled his fist around his eyes and mouthed Cry Baby. And then his lips curled up into a smirk and there...another unfamiliar jolt in my heart. Could it be because of the utter hatred? Considering my urge to hit him, it could be. But it didn't feel right. I somehow managed to roll my eyes at him and walked away stamping my feet on the floor. Yes, I absolutely hate him.

I untied my ponytail to let my hair loosen the hold of my heated head. 11-year-old Avni did not like him and I respect her feelings. I am completely aware of my childishness of holding grudges for something silly. He didn't even remember it. Maybe that's why I am mad at him. Now I want to play along and make sure he gives up before I do.

With that thought, I started washing the utensils in the kitchen. The colorful evening started embracing the dusk. A couple of guests stopped by for tea and snacks. Doctor Kaka, tired and sweaty, brought Nidhi back to her mother. And by the time Aai and Vahini went home, the only people left were Prachiti and her study group.

I sat on the sofa by the window, flipping through some catering contacts to send them a message. If I send 50 messages, at least a few of them will get back to me. I also told Nupur to enquire about catering whenever she gets any birthday cake orders. We've done events together in the past and this will give me the right direction to find leads.

I heard someone entering the café and thought it would be a customer, so I smiled before taking my eyes out of my diary for the person standing in front of me. Whatever little kindness I had in my heart turned into rivalry when I spotted the man smiling like a maniac at me.

"Hello there," Vihaan said cheekily, taking his hand out of his pocket and extending it towards me to shake it.

I brushed it away and shifted my focus back to the task at hand, refusing to look straight into his eyes. "What do you want? Are you here to make someone cry?"

"Actually, I am here to do exactly the opposite."

I swiftly turned the page of my diary before saying something really stupid. "Are you here to cry yourself?" And immediately regretted it.

"How can that be the opposite, dumbo?"

Dumbo? *Oh, the nerves.*

"Keep your nickname dictionary to yourself," I snapped at him, trying to intimidate him. But all he did was laugh and oh my, it was melodious.

Focus Avni.

"What do you want? Are you here to annoy me?"

"Not everything is about you. Don't feel so special," he replied, leaning against the counter.

"Excuse me?" I slammed the diary on the table and stood up from the sofa a little too quickly that my heel twitched, painfully twisting my ankle. I was going to fall to the floor when a strong arm held on to my waist to steady me. I grabbed the edge of the sofa and brushed away hair strands from my face to look at my evil savior. A pair of brown eyes met mine and for a moment I forgot where I was.

Vihaan raised his eyebrow at me, scanning my expressions, as I scanned his. He snapped his fingers in front of my face, "You okay?"

Oh god. I quickly adjusted myself and stepped away from him. "Yeah. Thanks." His gaze was still on me, on my eyes. I looked away only to face my guests. Prachiti's entire group was looking at us with silly smiles on their faces. I wished the floor would swallow me right there to bury my embarrassment. But as that didn't happen, I collected myself and smiled at Prachiti, "Do you need something, Prachiti?"

"No," she replied, trying to hide her giggle after witnessing my fall. "Vihaan Dada is here to help us with the project."

"Is that so?" I raised an eyebrow at him. He shoved his hands in his pocket and glanced between me and Prachiti.

"Yeah," Prachiti said. "Shall we? Vihaan Dada."

"Of course." He pulled an armchair to sit next to them and started explaining some tech concepts. The group of teenagers listened and watched as he demonstrated a diagram on Prachiti's laptop and helped them create pointers for the presentation. I wasn't planning to witness the whole thing. But I couldn't look away. I didn't want to miss it.

Vihaan answered every question the students asked and said something funny, making them all laugh. He himself was laughing, leaning against the armchair. How can someone look so good and so different? Do I look good to him? And, why exactly do I care? I should be working. But my heart kept drifting where it shouldn't.

"Thanks, Vihaan Dada," a boy from the group fist-bumped Vihaan. "That was pretty easy once you explained it."

"No need to thank me, buddy," he said. "Good luck with your group presentation."

Prachiti thanked Vihaan and packed her bag before meeting me by the counter to pay the bill. "Food was delicious, Avni Di. Thank you."

"You're welcome, Prachiti. Do visit again. Maybe we can discuss books."

"I'd love that," she declared with dreamy eyes.

The group waved me and Vihaan goodbye before walking down the lane to the bus stop. The cafe was chirping with their giggles for the entire evening and now it was just Vihaan and me.

Vihaan hovered near the counter for a moment and made his way towards the sofa. "Can I get two cups of adrak chai please?" he asked, looking at me.

"Two cups? What for?"

"That's not the right question to ask a customer!" I could see him hiding his smirk behind that stupidly handsome face.

"No need to be cocky, sir. I will get back right away." I smiled extra widely and made an effort to sound delightful. Rolling my eyes at him, I walked into the kitchen and returned with a teapot and two cups. "Here." I placed the tray in front of him and turned to leave.

"Sit with me, won't you?" The hint of softness in his voice almost startled me. I stopped in my tracks. Did he say what

I heard him say? "I'm sorry, what?"

"So now you have a hard time understanding language too." He poured tea into two cups and looked straight into my eyes. He waited for me to answer. His left eyebrow slightly raised.

"No, I understood it very well. I just didn't find it amusing." I folded my arms over my chest. "And stop teasing me. It's not funny anymore."

"I will stop," he nodded at the armchair opposite him for me to take a seat, "the day you stop being such a crybaby."

"Don't you dare call me that!"

"Then stop crying and have tea with me."

I opened my mouth several times to say something but couldn't utter a word. How do words abandon you in the middle of a war?

"Come on, Avni. Relax. Let's catch up over a cup of tea?"

Reasonable request, I guess.

I hesitated before sitting across from him on the armchair. He picked up a cup of tea and handed it over to me. I took it and had a sip of nice warm tea. The flavor of ginger refreshed my mind. A cup of tea to keep me sane.

"You did a good job with the place." Vihaan brought the teacup to his lips, blew it, and sipped. "I remember how it used to be."

"You do?" I didn't expect him to remember it after all these years. "It's been a long time since you were here."

"Yes. Harshad Dada had given me a couple of books back then. I still have those."

"Really? When did that happen?"

"The evening of the exam, he invited me in for a little chat and gave me some books."

I nodded. "Dada would make people read by creating interest for books, not just shoving a book in their hands."

"That's true." Vihaan nodded thoughtfully. "You make good tea, by the way. This is delicious," he said, taking the longest sip.

"Did you just compliment me?" I made a great show of sounding shocked.

He chuckled. "I did."

His eyes traveled everywhere inside the cafe, from bookshelves to the Reader's Corner to Avni's recommendation bookcase on the counter.

"You still have that?" He pointed at the bookcase.

"Wouldn't let it go," I said, remembering the time when I arranged books on that shelf for the first time, with Baba standing right beside me.

"That's nice." He genuinely smiled at me and I couldn't help but notice how good his smile made him look. I don't remember ever feeling captivated by a smile before.

"Thanks," I replied. To be honest, it was weird to chat with him. He is the same Vihaan from childhood, yet so different. I thought I wouldn't be able to talk to him freely. But he is easygoing. Casual and simple. We soon comforted into a normal conversation and it all felt good. I almost started to enjoy his company when he said, "Oh I gotta go. Duty calling."

He got up from his seat and I followed his suit, "Oh. Okay."

"I hope you are not still mad at me for what I said when I was 11," he held my gaze. "In my defense, I was a kid."

"I was a kid too. Easily emotional at times," I said and that made him laugh. I couldn't help but giggle.

He walked towards the counter and pulled out a wallet from the back pocket of his jeans, "Bill please."

"On the house," I declared. "You are Chaturvedi Ajoba's grandson and my very old rival. So..."

"I'm flattered," he said. "But I wouldn't." He handed me his credit card and waited for me to swipe it. When I returned his card with a print of the bill, he narrowed his eyes at me with a hint of a smirk.

"What?" I asked.

"I just remembered, before you started crying that day, you really wanted to smack me, didn't you?"

"No!"

"Yes! But instead, you started crying."

He was absolutely right. I really wanted to smack him for calling me dumb. But as I had no guts to do that, crying was the next best thing.

I bit my lower lip. "Honestly? Yes. But I couldn't. It was easier to cry."

"I remember Harshad Dada buying an ice cream for us, to patch things between us."

"No. That was to cheer me up and you didn't deserve it."

"Agreed. Please forgive me," he said dramatically, raising his hands in surrender.

"Consider it done in 2 to 5 business days," I declared.

He laughed, shoving his hands in his pockets. "By the way, does that ice cream stall still exists?"

"It does."

"Fantastic. I owe you an ice cream then," he offered. "To make it up to you.

I smiled and nodded. He walked towards the door, leaving me standing behind the counter. Then he stopped and looked back at me. "And Avni, as I said, I wasn't here to make anyone cry. I was here to put a smile on someone's face. The exact opposite you see."

"Really? And did you manage that?"

He just looked at me and jogged to his home...

SEVEN

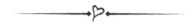

Growing up, I always had this image in my mind. One day my whole family would be seated in the garden of our bookstore. We would drink tea, chat, and laugh. I would make Onion Pakoras and we would all enjoy the evening breeze together. But today, sitting alone in the garden, I realized that when we wonder about our future, it's usually the fast-forwarded version of the present. But a lot of things change in between and nobody can control it. I lost my grandparents a few years ago, then my father and brother, and just like that, half of my family vanished before I got a chance to live my dream.

Today, when Baba's publisher paid a visit to my new café, saying "Arun sir would have been so proud of you," I almost cried in front of him.

Girish Kaka was Baba's one and only publisher. They were good friends. Baba trusted him with his manuscripts. Girish kaka still has a book inventory deal with us. Usually, his assistant sends the books. Today Girish Kaka himself arrived and said he would love to try something from my café's menu. He knows my family like his own. We drank Chai and talked about so many things for almost an hour, remembering the good old days.

After he left, I stayed in the garden to let my imagination bring back my lost family to me. Reliving some of the moments in my head that I don't ever want to get blurry. But it became unbearable and I had to leave before it got too overwhelming.

When I reached home, all my pets were already asleep. Harvey sensed my arrival and gave me a soft bark, before closing his eyes again. I kissed them all and went upstairs. On my way to my room, I saw movements on Nidhi's bed. I could see her tiny figure sitting on the bed in the dark.

"Hey, Nidhi." I flicked on the lamp and found her looking at me. "Couldn't sleep?"

"No." She whispered, "I'm scared."

I sat on her bed and pulled her on my lap, "Of what?"

"I don't really know," she replied, leaning into me.

"Okay. You don't have to be scared. I'm here now."

She wrapped her arms around me, not wanting to let me move. I pulled her even closer and kissed her forehead, "It's okay, Nidhi. I'm not going anywhere."

Slowly, she relaxed in my lap and demanded a bedtime story, and who could say no to her? Without wasting any second, I tucked her in and grabbed the book she wanted me to read.

By the time I reached the end of the story, her breathing was steady. I assumed she must have fallen asleep. But when I tried to move, she held my arm tightly and asked, "Is the bad man going to take our dogs away?"

"What? Who? The one from the story?"

"No," she whispered, snuggling closer to me. "The one Aai and Ajji were talking about. Is he going to take our dogs?"

"Oh Nidhi," I brushed my fingers through her soft hair. "Nobody is taking anything from us, okay? I promise."

"Then what were Aai and Ajji talking about?"

"Probably about the bad guy from the book they are reading."

"Really?"

"Of course. And you already know what happens to bad people."

"They turn green and ugly?"

I chuckled at her innocence. "Sure. Now go back to sleep. It's already past bedtime and you have to get up for school."

She hummed and gradually fell asleep in my arms. She looked so adorable. So innocent. I wished I could stay right there with her to make sure she won't be scared. What were Aai and Vahini talking about that scared Nidhi? I needed to know.

Carefully, I freed myself from her and tucked her in before going to my room. Sliding into my pajamas felt warm and comforting. And as much as my bed was looking divine, I fought back the urge to drop myself on the mattress and went downstairs to find Aai and Vahini. The house was empty, so the only possible place was the backyard. I made my way through the small passage to the garden and found two mothers sitting on armchairs.

"What are you two doing here?" I asked.

"Just talking," Vahini replied. "Did you eat dinner?"

I nodded and chased the topic that made my niece so worried. "Did something happen with Madhav Kaka again?"

Aai and Vahini stared at each other. I grabbed a chair and sat across from them. The weather was cold. Aai was wrapped up in her shawl. I pulled my legs to my chest and wrapped my arms around them to feel warm. "Aai? What is it?" I don't like to see these two women worried. Something obviously had happened that they weren't planning to tell me.

"Avu," Vahini said, "Aai received a phone call today. From Madhav Kaka."

Even though I was expecting it, my stomach dropped instantly. "About what?"

Did he tell her about the documents? Does Aai know he sent me those documents in the middle of the night? I wanted to ask but if that wasn't it, Aai would get more worried. I stayed quiet and let her continue.

"He wanted to know what have we decided. He said if we don't have money to pay him, we have to let him make decisions for the store." Aai paused. Her voice wobbled in her throat, "I'm worried that...that he might bring a buyer."

My heart started racing. I did not consider that possibility. Is it legally possible for him to do that? If yes, I didn't want to think about it.

"Tanvi and I have been thinking about it," Aai continued, "It's a big amount, Avu. We have to do something soon."

"I know Aai. I am searching for some catering gigs. I'll put 10 times more effort into the cafe and..."

Aai rested her hand on mine. "I'm not asking you or Tanvi to do anything. I already made a decision."

"What. I..." But Aai didn't let me finish.

"I'm breaking my Fixed Deposit. That amount will at least buy us some time until we arrange the rest of the money."

"No!" I almost yelled and sat straight. "No way. You are not going to do that."

"We have to do something, Avu," Aai pleaded.

"And we will. But not this way."

"You are so young, full of dreams. Book Cafe means a lot to you and I want you to focus on it and let me worry about the money." Aai dabbed her eyes.

"And I want the exact thing for you. I don't want anyone to worry about anything. I know I can do this, Aai."

"I'm not doubting that. But..."

"And what if..." I interrupted her, "What if you give him money and he still keeps bugging us? How do you know he is going to stop after that?"

Vahini nodded thoughtfully. Aai looked down in her lap, anxiously twisting the corner of her shawl.

"People who are after money are always after money, Aai," I said. "That's the only thing they care about, not the emotions. You would give them everything you have, yet they wouldn't care. They feel entitled and that's not good for anyone. We have to think this through."

She considered my thoughts.

"Besides," I added, "I find it odd that, after all these years, he wants money now. Something must have happened. Otherwise, why would he show up to claim his rights out of the blue?"

Both Aai and Vahini looked at me with concern spread across their faces.

I continued, "You can trust me, Aai. I can do something."

"We know that, Avu. But..."

"Don't worry Aai," I interrupted her, just like Baba used to say when he wanted everyone to get along with his plan so that no one would suffer. "Let's go inside. It's cold out here."

Aai sighed and stood up. Vahini was still not sure what decision was made.

I faced both of them and said, "And if you two decide to talk about Madhav Kaka, make sure Nidhi isn't around."

Tanvi Vahini let out a small gasp, "Did she hear it?"

"Not all of it. But enough to make her feel insecure."

Vahini's face fell. She looked miserable and I regretted every word I said. But this can't happen again and they need to know how fragile Nidhi is. Her heart is so pure. She is not old enough to know how grownups play different games than children.

"I thought she was asleep," Vahini whispered anxiously. I put my arm around her shoulder to comfort her. "Vahini, don't overthink this. She is fine. We read the story and she is sleeping right now."

Once inside the house, I made another effort to brush their worries away, "Let's have some coffee."

Both of them smiled and nodded.

On my way to the kitchen, I found Nidhi walking down the stairs, rubbing her eyes, "Where did you go Avu Attu? I was waiting for you."

"Aww. Come here." I lifted her in my arms and softly hugged her to assure her that she is not alone. She would never be alone. "Would you like some hot chocolate?"

"Really? Is Aai allowing it?"

I chuckled, "She won't mind."

I carefully put her down on the kitchen counter and made coffee for grownups and hot chocolate for my little niece. The smell of chocolate lightened up her eyes, filling my heart with so much love.

"Let's go." I let her carry the tray, which was as big as her, and we made our way to the living room to find our mothers sitting quietly.

"Aai, where were you?" Nidhi walked to her mother and held the tray, "I've brought coffee for you and Ajji."

"You made it?" Vahini asked and my niece nodded, then looked at me guiltily.

"Nidhi made it all, isn't she a big girl now?" I winked at her and her whole face smiled at me.

All of us sat around the tea table. Nidhi snuggled next to her mother and enjoyed her hot chocolate. We didn't talk much. It was a comfortable silence. Nobody needed to say anything. Everybody respected each other's silence. Just being there together expressed more than words could ever do.

I put my empty coffee cup down on the table and slumped back on the sofa. Aai did the same and looked at Nidhi, "How about story night?"

Little Nidhi screamed in excitement. "Yes. I want story night," she demanded to her Ajji.

There was a time when my Ajji used to tell us all a story. Ajoba, Baba, Harshad Dada, me, and Aai would sit around her and she would tell a mythological story. Every time something new and equally interesting. During summer, we would spread mattresses on the terrace of the house to spend the night with Ajji's story as soothing as a lullaby. That was the best time. And now, my Aai is the Ajji of the house and Nidhi is the child with dreamy eyes.

Aai pulled Nidhi on her lap and kissed her forehead. "Today, I'll tell a story from Mahabharata."

"Ajji please," Nidhi rolled her eyes. "Why can't you just tell normal princess stories?"

It made us all burst out laughing, that's how she shifts our moods.

"This story is also about the princess," Aai confirmed. "Princess of Panchal, Draupadi."

"Alright. I allow it," Nidhi said, resting her head on my mother's chest. "Is she pretty?"

"Prettier than your beloved Elsa," Aai said, wrapping her arms around Nidhi.

Vahini and I cleared the living room, shifted the tea table to the side, and spread out some mattresses on the floor.

Once Nidhi was comfortable on the mattress, we all settled down around her.

"Once upon a time, King of Panchal organized a sacred fire *Yajna*. And a princess was born from fire. She was so beautiful, so fierce, so unique..."

My mother began the tale of Draupadi's childhood and our story night began. Nidhi listened to the story with awe, asked hundreds of questions, yawned loudly, and finally fell asleep in her grandma's lap.

EIGHT

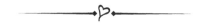

Our story night extended till 3 in the morning. While everyone comforted into the night and fell asleep, I stayed wide awake. Nothing calmed my mind. Eventually, I went upstairs to my room to quietly think about how I can arrange at least half the amount Madhav Kaka is asking. There's no point in checking my account. Whatever little amount I had saved with my catering contracts, I used most of it for my café. I'm left with the bare minimum but I don't want Aai or Vahini to worry about money. I might be clueless right now, but I'll think about something.

My room was slightly colder than downstairs. A soft noise of rain was filling the quietness. I flicked on the table lamp and stood next to my window for a while, watching raindrops form clusters on the glass of my window. Each droplet brought back tons of memories.

When I was young, Baba sometimes used to read me poems when it rained. I used to sit on his lap facing rainfall and he would let verses from the poem float in the air. He had handwritten his favorite poems in a diary. Baba had separate diaries for so many things. One to write notes about his own books, one to keep track of bookstore expenses, one to write his personal things, and one for poems. That's how I learned to keep a diary for different things. I hardly write anything personal in my diary anymore, only notes and to-do lists. Baba used to write quite often. All his thoughts used to be organized neatly on paper.

By the end of each year, he would keep his diaries in a briefcase on the loft. None of us have gathered the courage to go through Baba and Dada's personal things yet. We did donate some of their clothes, but some things would never be easy to open. I do have his last diary with me. A few days after he was gone, when I was hovering near Baba's desk, I found his diary. His fountain pen was tucked between the pages and the diary was only half-filled. Those were the last thoughts he ever wrote. I kept it with me hoping I would meet my Baba again in those pages, even for a short time. But I have never read a single page yet.

I walked over to my cupboard and found a stack of my diaries along with Baba's diary. I picked it up and settled on my bed.

My hand shook when I tried to open his diary. His thoughts. His handwriting. The smell of the ink. I wanted to clutch it close yet keep it away, afraid to stumble across memories. The matte black cover was Baba's favorite. All his diaries were black. The one in my hand had 2018 embossed on it in golden color. I reluctantly opened the first page and began reading.

~

Jan 5, 2018

The New Year's celebration was amazing this year. Harsh and Avni organized a beautiful event at the bookstore. A lot of readers and the entire Rhythm Lane were invited. I'm still processing the last year when the new one is already running faster ahead.

So many things happened last year. Avni has already completed two years of Culinary arts degree. She is so happy about it as by the time she graduates, she will be ready to start the café. I can't wait to see what she has planned for the book café. She was so little when she said she wants to start a café one day. Time flies so fast.

Harsh, my son, became a father. Yes, Amrita and I have been promoted to Ajji and Ajoba. Little Nidhi looks just like Tanvi. But her eyes are like Harshad. Our house is filled with joy with the arrival of a beautiful baby girl. She will soon turn 1.

The bookstore has done good business last year. I also finished the first draft of my new book. So yes, so many things happened last year and are carried forward into the new one.

For this year, my goal is to start preparing for Avni's café. I had already started saving some money and I will continue to do so until she graduates. I want to finish my book, take a break and play with my granddaughter. And, this year, I'm planning to take everyone on a small vacation. It's been years since we all went somewhere. It'll be a memorable trip.

~

I couldn't read any further. The vacation never happened. Baba didn't get the chance to see my bookstore. It's so unfair. The bookstore meant a lot to him and now Madhav Kaka might take it all away if I don't arrange the money.

I don't want to think about any of this. I miss my Baba and Dada so much. Why did God take them away from me? I don't want to be alone.

I closed Baba's diary and kept it aside. The clock struck 5:15 in the morning. I didn't realize when the dusk turned into dawn. On the wall clock, the minute hand circled across the numbers and snatched another minute away from me. I have so little time left to arrange money that a ticking clock has started terrifying me. Every passing second is pushing me closer to the deadline. But I have to bury my fears deep down so I can focus on important things.

To distract myself, I grabbed my daily planner and opened the last page where I have been jotting down ideas for my cafe for months.

Things to do for café-

1. Create and print a menu card (Done)

2. Launch social media pages for the cafe (Done)

3. Print and circulate pamphlets

4. Start another book club

5. Launch a website? (Brainstorm ideas)

6. Start a Nook for work-from-cafe and writer's corner for authors

7. More chairs for the garden

Oh, yes. The nooks for Work-from-café and Writer's corner. I remember writing it down and thinking how cool it would be to have a community of people. They can work from the cafe and I can provide a relaxing environment and food. Authors can spend time writing and reading among the bookshelves and how amazing it would be to have them in a book club.

I scratched my head wondering, isn't now a good time to start these nooks? It is, isn't it?

Everything about that idea felt right at the moment. Even though a wave of anxiety washed over me, I didn't let it take control. I want to do everything for the business, even if things are uncertain.

I powered on my laptop and opened a DIY graphic designing website to create a social media post for both the nooks. The site had so many ready-made aesthetic templates. I chose one that I liked and added the text to the graphic.

"'Bored of work from home? Enjoy a fun & vibrant work environment with delicious food, refreshing chai, and the friendly company of dogs. Visit Among The Pages today!"

Okay. Looks nice!

I downloaded the image and scheduled it to be posted on both Facebook and Instagram at 8 a.m.

Outside, the dawn sprinkled soft colors over the horizon. I got up from my bed and opened the window to inhale the fresh air. The rain had left the fragrance of moist soil behind. Soon, the Sun would cast a golden glow on the city and the night's blue would be long gone. *I hoped so.*

I pulled a chair and sat facing the window to leaf through my oldest and messiest Recipe Diary from the stack. It has all my favorite recipes I have tried over the years. It's been a while since I last opened this diary. It's a treasure of flavors of different kinds. A wave of nostalgia hummed through my veins as I turned pages after pages of recipes. There are notes scribbled across the margins. Colorful post-it notes with lists of ingredients and spices. Aai's homemade masala recipes, and Ajji's special Indian snacks.

I flicked through the instructions and came across oil stains and turmeric fingerprints on pages. Tucking my hair behind both ears, I shortlisted a few recipes to include in my catering portfolio.

I'll look at everything as an opportunity and work extra hard for my family. I can somehow manage catering gigs and café together. Whatever it takes to arrange the money.

With that thought, I heaved myself from the chair to get ready for the day. A long shower with my extended hair wash routine refreshed me. I changed into a nice warm purple t-shirt with a delicate floral design around the neck and sleeves. Pairing it with a denim skirt, I unwrapped my hair from the towel and slumped on my bed to check my phone. There were too many Instagram notifications. It has never happened before. The post I had scheduled must have gotten uploaded.

And my goodness. 120 likes, 4 story shares, 3 follows, a couple of comments, and 2 DMs inquiring about the nooks.

I went through each notification one by one. Out of 4 story shares, 2 were by Rutu and Nupur. One was Tanvi Vahini. And the 4th share, to my total disbelief and delight, was by Vihaan Chaturvedi.

Check out this new book cafe. Perfect to spend a couple of hours working with the best cup of tea you'll ever have. Vihaan had written and tagged the page in his Instagram Story.

I honestly was not expecting that. Rutu, Nupur, and I share updates about our businesses on each other's social media all the time. It was no surprise they would do it. But Vihaan? It's a simple gesture but it meant a lot.

Before replying to him, I checked the 2 DMs. One of the messages was from a girl named Shweta.

"Hi, Avni. Remember me? My friend and I had breakfast at your café before our presentation a couple of days ago. FYI, it went amazingly well. My entire team wants to see your book café and we are interested to know about the Work-From-Café nook that you posted."

The girl had mentioned that she would bring her whole team to my café. I quickly typed back a reply.

"Hi Shweta, that's amazing. Congratulations. I would love to meet your team. Do visit anytime and we can arrange your nook. Have a good day!"

Once I re-shared all the story responses on the café's page, I switched to my personal Instagram and found a follow request from the same boy with brown eyes and shiny hair.

I accepted Vihaan's follow request, followed him back from my personal page, and sent him a DM.

"Hey. Thanks for re-sharing my posts. Really appreciate it."

Within moments, three dots appeared, followed by his reply. "Don't mention it. Good idea, by the way, even I might try the nook."

"Oh, of course. Anytime. Thanks again," I typed and sent.

I stared at the screen. It was the first time I was texting Vihaan and it felt oddly different. *Good different.* I didn't even realize I was smiling until Aai's sudden appearance startled me and I almost dropped my phone on my face. "Why are you smiling like that?"

"Aai? When did you come upstairs?"

"Just in time to see you lying on the bed after a shower and smiling into the phone screen."

I immediately jumped out of the bed and stood next to her, "Better?"

"Not yet. Blow-dry your hair and comb them well. Or bring your hairbrush downstairs, I'll do it. And how many times do I have to tell you not to lie in bed with wet hair?"

"Sorry Aai," I gave her a bone-crushing hug and kissed her cheek. She hates it when I leave a mark of lip gloss or lipstick. On any normal day, Aai would have wiped out that kiss. But today she let it be.

"Come downstairs for breakfast, Tanvi has made your favorite."

"Okay."

Aai smiled at me and went downstairs. I looked into the mirror to get ready and found bags under my eyes. That won't go away so easily. But I managed to somewhat hide them with makeup and hurried downstairs with my bag.

As soon as I entered the kitchen, a mesmerizing aroma of Idli Sambar rumbled through my stomach.

"Avu. Here," Vahini said, serving me 2 Idlis dipped in a bowl full of Sambar and Chutney. She knows how I like it.

Giving my Vahini a quick hug, I grabbed the bowl and bit into the luscious Idli. The flavors danced against my tongue, making me close my eyes with delight.

"So delicious," I mumbled and blew a chef kiss to my Vahini before making my way to the living room. Nidhi was sitting in her favorite bean bag again and it almost consumed her entirely. She was busy finishing her last-minute homework and Aai was feeding her breakfast.

"Morning Nidhi," I pulled her cheek.

"Attu. Don't disturb me," she ordered. "I forgot to finish homework."

Aai and I both giggled. "Sorry, Madam."

She quickly scribbled her pending homework while eating Idli and shoved the notebook in her Frozen-themed bag.

"Done!" she declared with a smile.

"Bravo," I said. "Now can I talk?"

"But you shouldn't when you are eating," she replied, opening her mouth to take another bite of Idli from her Ajji.

I shook my head and let her finish breakfast in peace. If I talk, she would be late for school and Vahini will have a near-breakdown experience.

So instead, I focused on enjoying breakfast. Vahini joined us with a plate for herself and sat on the chair.

"Sambar is delicious, Tanvi," Aai said to her with a smile.

"Truly," I added with a mouthful.

"Thank you," she beamed and served some more sambar to all of us.

"Avu," Aai said, finishing the last few bites of Idli.

"Hmm?"

"Tanvi's parents called some time ago."

"Oh. How are they?"

"Good," Vahini replied. "They want to meet us."

"So Tanvi and I were thinking to travel to Panvel this afternoon to see her parents. And…" Aai waited for me to register everything and continued, "We might have to stay for a couple of days. Do you think you can manage here? Or else…"

"Of course, Aai," I replied. "I can handle everything here. You know I have lived alone before," I smiled reassuringly.

"Yes, Avu," Vahini added. "But that doesn't mean we won't be worried. Are you sure you'd be okay for a couple of days?"

"Don't worry, Vahini. I'll be fine." I sipped a spoonful of sambar and further asked, "How are you planning to go then?"

"Tanvi has booked bus tickets for Nidhi and two of us," Aai replied. "We would be leaving after lunch."

"Okay." I nodded, finishing the last bite of breakfast.

Vahini's face wasn't her usual relaxed face. She was trying her best to not look worried. But her attempts weren't successful.

"Vahini? Everything okay?"

She sighed with concern and took a seat next to me. "You know my Baba. He doesn't take proper care of his health. I think he just wants to see me. But I'm planning to take him to the doctor while I'm there."

"Yes. Maybe you can bring them here. It'll be a nice change for them."

Vahini nodded thoughtfully.

I gave her a reassuring hug. Her face broke into a soft smile that didn't quite reach her eyes. I wish I could do something to make her feel better. But she won't feel good until she sees her parents.

"Stay home to pack your bags," I said to both of them.

"We will stop by the cafe before leaving," Aai replied, packing Nidhi's school bag.

"Okay Aai, I will cook some light food for your journey and pack it for you."

Aai smiled and brushed her fingers through my hair with love and said, "At least comb your hair nicely, Avu."

"Aai!" I rolled my eyes. "Anything else?"

Vahini giggled when Aai said, "Nothing. Just don't forget to lock the front door every night. Harvey is the only one with sharp eyes."

"I'm not a child, Aai," I said, keeping my plate in the sink. "I'll be alright."

She shook her head, not believing a word I said. So I picked up my bag, gave Nidhi a quick peck on the cheeks, and hurried to the book cafe.

NINE

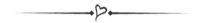

"Travel safe. Call me when you reach." I waved at my family from outside the book cafe. It took a lot of effort to convince Nidhi that I won't be joining them on the journey to Panvel. That I have to open the book cafe every day and who would look after dogs? But she was pretty upset and started insisting she would stay here with me. It took three of us to bribe her with a new hairband and a promise to buy ice cream if she agreed to travel.

I stood on the patio staring at the road until my family was out of my sight. When I went inside, everything was awfully quiet. For a moment, I considered running after my family to join them. But all I could do at the moment was to put on some music and get back to work.

Taking my seat behind the counter, I powered on the computer and opened my diary in front of me. I sent a follow-up message to work-from-cafe inquiries and received a positive reply. Shweta said she and her team will stop by this week. And before they arrive, I need to be prepared with the pricing package for daily, weekly, and monthly bookings.

I twisted a strand of hair in my fingers and read through my notes. I want people to find this place relaxing and budget-friendly at the same time. Overcharging may pay bills, but it won't make customers happy. Food bill plus a small amount for table reservation makes sense. I scribbled some more notes and created social media posts for the week.

As I was designing the posts, snow-white fur tickled against my legs. Cookie's small head popped right next to the counter. She looked at me with intent, seeking attention.

"Hey Cookie." I brushed my fingers on her forehead. "Are you missing Nidhi?"

She woofed, jumped on my lap, and curled into a bundle.

"Aww. I miss her too. But she's gone for just a couple of days okay?"

She didn't make any noise. I let her snuggle in my lap for as long as she wanted. My other three pets were laying lazily on the rug in the Reader's Corner. They must be missing the absence of three people too.

I checked the time on my ancient computer. The bottom right corner flicked from 3:05 to 3:06. Time flew quite fast since the morning. I closed my diary and pulled Cookie closer into a hug. She comforted in my embrace by resting her head on my chest.

The lack of sleep was making my eyes burn. I needed to close them for a while. Tiredness was catching up to me. A mini nap might solve all my problems. I slowly leaned forward to rest my head on the counter and closed my eyes. Every sound and movement around me started feeling like a blur of activities. I didn't have the energy to open my eyes.

The sleep I didn't get at night started breaking free. I could feel my eyelids getting heavy. Wall-clock ticked somewhere over my head. I could hear a soft muffle of tree leaves and the steady breathing of Cookie in my lap. Everything else was fading away. At some point, Cookie leapt from my lap to join her companions in the Reader's

Corner. I opened my eyes into a slit to make sure my pets were okay but soon fell back asleep, I don't know for how long. After a while, the doorbell chimed. Or did I imagine it? I didn't move an inch, not until I heard someone clear their throat. "Is the cafe open?"

I think so. I'm not sure anymore. I could use some more sleep if you could just wait for a couple of minutes.

"Avni?" I heard the voice again. This can't be a dream. The voice was too real. Vihaan?

I tried to rub all the sleep out of my eyes and held the edge of the counter to stand up and greet the guest in front of me. A familiar face. But so blurry. So misplaced. I blinked several times. Everything was shaking and spinning around me.

I pushed the chair away and put one foot in front of the other to walk ahead. The floor beneath me felt weird, like a pit, and it was getting closer. How?

"Hey hey." Vihaan rushed to hold me in his arms. "Are you okay? What's wrong?"

I don't know what's wrong. Everything was fine some time ago. I was just taking a nap, wasn't I?

I closed my eyes to block the world from spinning. I could feel the strong arm wrapped tightly around my shoulder, pinning me into place so I won't lose balance. A moment later, I was in the armchair. Soft and comfy. Much better than the chair behind the counter.

"Avni?" Vihaan pressed his palm on my forehead to check if I had a fever. "Open your eyes. Are you okay? Should I call Doctor Kaka?"

When I tried to move, my neck was hurting. I slowly lifted my heavy eyelids and blinked rapidly to adjust to the light. The world wasn't spinning anymore. And nothing was out of place. Vihaan's handsome face was right in front of me, his eyebrows frowned. He looked good. So good, I wanted to hold his face in my hands. I blinked and drew a deep breath. The dizziness was getting washed away, slowly.

"Are you feeling alright?" he asked, impatient to hear my response.

"I guess so," I muttered under my breath. "What happened here?"

"I think you are tired."

"What time is it?" I asked, rubbing my hands on my face.

"Nearly 5"

"What? It was 3 when I last checked."

"You must have fallen asleep."

"I just wanted to take a nap," I replied, annoyed with myself. "And..."

"It's okay," he said softly. "Nothing happened here."

I buried my face in my palms and groaned. It was very irresponsible of me to fall asleep. I shouldn't have.

"When was the last time you ate?" Vihaan asked.

"Oh...um...I ate a sandwich for breakfast and then..."

And then nothing. I remembered packing snacks for my family and waving them goodbye. I had planned to eat lunch after they left but I forgot.

"That's why you almost fainted." Vihaan's voice was full of concern. He looked into my eyes and sighed. "Your eyes are tired, Avni. You need to eat. Wait right here. I'll bring something."

"No no," I tried to get up from the armchair. But as if the armchair had arms tied around me, I sank back down. "Oh."

Vihaan chuckled, "Don't worry. I will make something warm and nice. Trust me." He gave a reassuring smile and went to the kitchen.

I rested my head on the back of the chair and closed my eyes. My throbbing head desperately needed some tea.

Adrak Chai can fix any problems, especially headaches. I'll make some tea later, once I eat.

Something in my kitchen dropped to the floor. A loud noise echoed outside.

"You okay in there?" I asked. Letting someone else in my kitchen was probably the bravest thing for me. Mostly because I was too tired to move.

"Yeah, sorry. All good," came a shaky reply.

After a few minutes, Vihaan walked out of the kitchen carrying a tray. He placed it on the table and sat on the chair next to me. I sat up straight and scanned the contents on the tray. Two bowls of instant Maggi noodles with extra cheese and 2 cups of tea, which I assumed had ginger in it because the smell itself was refreshing.

Vihaan hesitated before handing me a bowl of Maggi Noodles. "This is all I can make," he said.

"It's okay. I like Maggi."

I held the bowl in my palms and instantly felt warm. "What about you?" I asked when Vihaan didn't pick up his bowl.

"You first," he said.

"Are you experimenting your cooking skills on me?"

"Maybe." He smiled.

"Good God. Okay." I poked the noodles with the fork, "Hm. Nicely cooked," and stuffed my mouth with a big bite. The melted cheese made a beautiful umbrella on it, with a sprinkle of chili flakes and oregano. The boy knows stuff. "Good Good," I said, "I'm impressed."

He chuckled and grabbed a bite himself. I picked up the tea from the tray. "Alright. Smells good. Let's see if it tastes as good."

I lifted the cup and brought it to my lips. The aroma of ginger went straight into my head and I felt better even before I took the sip. See? Tea works like magic. Slightly blowing it, I took a long sip. And I must say, it wasn't bad at all. "Nice," I mumbled and closed my eyes as I inhaled the aroma.

"Really?"

I almost forgot he was sitting right there.

"I mean. Um, a bit more sugar would have been good. But nice job."

"Your reaction told me that it's pretty good. But okay, have your moment," he chuckled. "It's fine as long as you eat and feel better."

Oh! Alright.

We sat there, eating a bowl of Maggi and sipping tea. Having Vihaan next to me felt... well, nice.

"You think I can make this tea for my grandparents? Would they like it?" he asked, glancing down at his teacup.

"Of course, they will," I replied between a mouthful of noodles.

"They love your chai. I sometimes think they love you more than they love me."

"Of course, they love me more," I teased. "And I can teach you how to brew nice tea. The key is to let ginger and lemongrass simmer well into the water with tea."

He chuckled, "sounds good."

I felt energized as I finished my bowl of noodles and tea. A sudden loud bark of Harvey filled the room. My pets woke up from their nap and rushed to greet me.

One by one, I pampered them until they were happy and wide awake. "Meet our new guest," I said to all four of them. "This is Vihaan. Chaturvedi Ajoba's grandson."

They all turned their heads toward him and scanned his face. *Fine hooman, since you are related to Chaturvedi Ajoba, you are welcome here.*

"He is a friend," I said to Cookie as she jumped on my lap. "Nothing to worry about."

She barked at him to make conversation.

"Hey," he said to her, somewhat awkwardly.

I laughed. "You've never talked with dogs, have you?"

"I have. But not recently. And suddenly there are four of them. One particularly scary," he said, looking at Harvey the German shepherd.

"Don't worry. They are harmless. Until of course, if you do some harm to me, then you better run."

He met my gaze and arched an eyebrow. "I wouldn't dare."

"Good."

Stevey walked towards him and wiggled his tail, which is a compliment. Vihaan carefully placed his palm on Stevey's forehead and patted it. That made Charlie feel insecure. *I want attention too.* He jumped on the sofa next to Vihaan with his tongue hanging out. *Hello, nice to meet you.*

"Hey, buddy. Glad you like me." Vihaan held his palm in front of Charlie and he put his paw on it.

Harvey couldn't care less, but he'll come around. He likes to observe people before offering his valuable friendship.

Vihaan and I played with my pets, chatted with them, and laughed over silly things dogs do to seek attention. The cafe started feeling lively and happy. My head wasn't hurting anymore and I felt better. Good, rather. Pretty good.

Vihaan slowly got comfortable around my pets. He even tried to get Cookie to shake his hand and she wasn't anxious anymore. I'm glad he finally met my pets.

As we were chatting, customers entered the cafe. I quickly stood up to greet the two girls of my age, leaving Vihaan with my pets.

The girls were from Rutu's hostel and wanted a couple of books, which I'm proud to say that I had in my inventory. Both hard and soft covers. "We would love your suggestions on books," one of them said. "Meanwhile, a cup of lemongrass tea would be nice."

"Of course. I would recommend sitting in the Reader's Corner. You can browse books. I'll be right there to help you."

The girls made their way to the Reader's Corner, smiling at my pets.

"Can you stay with them?" I asked Vihaan. "I'll just..."

"Of course." He nodded, ruffling Charlie's head.

I brewed the lemongrass tea and carried it to the Reader's Corner. The girls were shuffling through the stack of books they had shortlisted. I had a nice chat with them, suggested some fun reads, and printed their bill of 3 books and the tea.

When the girls left with happy faces, I found Vihaan in the garden playing with my pets. He was having a good time with them. His attempt of getting along with Harvey made me smile.

"Hey," I joined him. "Thanks for looking after them."

"You know what?" he smiled. "I think even Harvey likes me now. We are bonding."

"Really? Hearty Congratulations. Tea to celebrate?"

"Sure."

"Would you like to eat something? I'm still hungry. Thought I'll make something."

"Yeah. Whatever you are having." He threw a ball at my pets and watched as they fiddled with it with their paws. Cookie struggled to get hold of the ball for herself. And when she couldn't she just walked to the side and sat down. I gave her a gigantic hug before making my way to the kitchen.

Putting tea to brew, I made Cheesy Potato Rolls with Chutney on the side. Serving it on two plates and pouring tea that I made with extra effort into two cups, I walked back outside to join Vihaan.

"Here," I handed him the plate and teacup, "Special Amrutatulya Chai with Potato Roll."

His fingers brushed over mine when he took the cup from me and our eyes met. That simple touch shot a wave of electricity through my skin. I don't know if I was imagining it, but the way he looked at me flipped my heart for real. I shook my head and focused on the meal.

"Delicious," he said, taking a bite.

"Thanks," I smiled, biting into the goodness of cheese.

Cookie looked at me with eyes cute and round as a button. Of course, how could I forget? I kept my plate down and filled 4 bowls with dog food. Cookie's whole face lightened up and she barked to tell others. *It's time to eat.*

I kept their bowls next to my chair on the patio and we all resumed our evening tea and snack party.

"How come you have so many dogs?" Vihaan asked, watching them all with curiosity and affection.

"They are all rescued," I informed. "My Baba brought Stevey home on my 17th birthday, from the rescue shelter. Harvey joined the family a year later, Charlie a couple of years after Harvey. And Cookie here is just 2 years old."

He looked at them with a smile on his face.

"The shelter knows us very well," I told him. "We often volunteer there. Baba used to donate money to the shelter. We still do it whenever we can."

"That's great," he gave me a smile that was not his regular one. This one was different. Good, but different. As if he was trying to understand every little part of my life.

"Want anything else to eat?" I asked him to fill the silence.

"Oh, no. I should get going."

"Alright," I replied, glancing at my phone. It was only 6:30. I should stay here for at least 2 more hours. But today I didn't have the energy. And the thought of having an early night felt divine.

"I was thinking, I'll go home too," I mumbled to myself, keeping empty plates and cups back on the tray.

"Come on then," he said. "I'll walk you home."

"Oh no. You don't have to. I can manage."

"It's no big deal," he insisted again. "And you still seem tired."

I didn't know what to say. He was probably being friendly, but I liked the way he cared.

"Okay," I gave in. "Let me just clean up."

He nodded and helped me pack up. While I rinsed everything, he locked the back door and brought my pets inside, and held their leashes, except Cookie who was still unsure about him. She decided to stick with me, her second favorite human being, after Nidhi.

Locking the front door, we all walked to my home. The road ahead was peacefully quiet. Only a few people and vehicles passed by us. I stole a glance at my tall companion.

"What?" he asked when he sensed my gaze.

"Nothing. Just wanted to say thank you."

"For what?"

"For being there...and.."

He smiled, still looking ahead. We walked in silence until we were outside my house.

"Bye then," I said as I unlocked the gate.

"Goodnight, Avni," he replied and folded his arms over his chest.

I hovered near the gate for a moment before getting inside the house. Once my dogs were in, I waved at Vihaan one last time and locked the door.

He was still standing outside. When I sneaked a peek through the window curtain, he started walking back towards Rhythm Lane, taking one last look in my house's direction.

Did he just wait till I was safely inside the house?

TEN

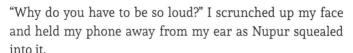

"Why do you have to be so loud?" I scrunched up my face and held my phone away from my ear as Nupur squealed into it.

"Listen," she ignored me and continued. "We have an event to cater." I could hear her flipping pages of a notebook and scribbling something down.

"What's the event?" I asked, sitting straight on my bed.

"A friend of mine is hosting a mini party for her younger sister's graduation. Roughly 20 people. They need a cake, some cupcakes, and snacks."

"That's perfect. "I'll share my new catering portfolio." I suddenly felt energized.

"Yes, I'll forward it to her. Will call you once she gets back to me."

"Okay cool," I replied. "Thank you so much, Nupur."

"No problem. We'll make sure their party goes well," she said with enthusiasm and hung up the call.

I kept my phone on top of the side drawer and let out a sigh of relief. After sending out so many messages, I at least have one catering order to look forward to. It won't earn me much, but it's exactly what I need to boost my confidence.

Leaning against the headboard of my bed, I watched as a thin layer of clouds ran across the slice of the moon. The night was slowly embracing the quietness. I pulled my blanket closer to my chest and grabbed Baba's diary.

I have been brushing through his diary every night, careful not to get captivated by memories. He has written about his book progress, his plans for the next few years, new book ideas, and about him missing his parents. Some entries are dedicated to my cooking attempts that he used to love. Baby Nidhi was almost on every page. Feb 2018 entries are all about him and Dada planning to attend the literary event. I read and re-read some entries and paused when I stumbled across an entry from March.

~

March 7, 2018

My new book, a story of a family from the 1947 era has got a good response from publisher and beta readers. But it needs a lot of edits, which is what I'll be doing for an entire month. Now I don't have to worry about the bookstore. Avni and Harsh are handling the store very well. Avni spends her evening after college at the bookstore and lets Harsh take a break. I drop by once in a while to make sure the kids have all they need. Otherwise, I spend my time writing and playing with my granddaughter. When I call her from the doorway, she gives me a bright smile and claps her hands. Amrita and I spend our afternoons babysitting Nidhi so Tanvi can take a break. Amrita tells her stories and baby Nidhi sleeps on my lap. It's a beautiful feeling.

This evening, Harsh and Tanvi took baby Nidhi for her vaccination. And Avni was busy with her college assignments. So I spent the evening in the store. And now, I am glad that nobody was there but me. Because Madhav Bhau stopped by. I thought he just wanted to chat. But he was trying to convince me to do something that I'd never do. He wants me to sell the bookstore to a potential buyer who is willing to offer good money. I told him that's not why I started the store, I don't want to sell it. But he started explaining to me about property prices and how we'll all benefit from selling the book house.

I should have listened to my father. He knew Madhav Bhau wasn't interested in helping or running the bookstore. He just wanted an investment option. That's why taking money from family members is not always a good idea. You think you know your people until the money comes in between your relationship.

I'm glad I added Amrita, Harsh, and Avni as business successors years ago. If something happens to me, Harsh and Avni will have the bookstores to themselves. For now, Madhav Bhau stopped bugging me. But I suspect he'll pitch the idea again.

~

For the first time, I came across an entry where Baba mentioned Madhav kaka, and not in a good way. Now I'm well aware of Madhav Kaka's intentions. It's all about money for him and nothing else. I tried to read a few more pages to find out if there was anything else about Madhav Kaka. But I couldn't read through some of the happy yet painful memories. Baba's life was all about his family. He loved everyone so much. He always cared about others before himself.

Tears that I had held for a long time escaped my eyes. I lay on my bed, remembering the time when my father and brother were always around me. How my life was colorful with them. It's been four years, yet the wounds on our hearts are fresh. Time might heal everything. It might hurt a little less. But nothing can bring them back to me and that's never going to be easy.

The first year of losing them, we were all so lost in our thoughts, I don't even remember what we all did. Aai used to spend as much time with Nidhi as possible. Reading and cooking kept me occupied. Vahini, almost every day, organized bookshelves from scratch. Nidhi kept her smiling once in a while, but it was painful to watch her go through parenthood without Dada by her side.

Almost a year and a half later, when I took Vahini with me to a nearby temple, she wept and said, "Sometimes I feel, it should have been me. Not him. But that's selfish. What would he have done without me? If it wasn't for Nidhi, I don't think I would have lived. Nidhi is all I have…"

That day, it sank on me how much lonely she was. Aai and I decided that we would never leave Vahini alone. Together, we somehow managed to survive.

I wiped my eyes, took some deep breaths to calm down, and closed my eyes. I don't remember the exact time I fell asleep. But when I woke up the next morning, it took me a moment to realize where I was, and most importantly, I was alone. Home outside my bedroom door, which usually is filled with Nidhi's chirping, felt awfully quiet. I went downstairs to check on my pets. They must have felt lonely too. I should have put their beds in my room.

All of them turned their sleepy heads in my direction as they heard my footsteps coming downstairs. Cookie snuggled out of her soft blanket and ran towards me. I crouched down to pick her up in my arms and sat between my pets to adore them. They jumped around me as I played with them while my morning tea was brewing. We all spent some time in the garden.

Letting them wander around in the house, I got ready for the day. My phone blinked with a text from Vahini. "We reached safely last night. Will call you soon. Take care." I typed back a quick reply, "Okay. You too take care." And with my pets by my side, I walked to Rhythm Lane, ready to unfold the day without losing my mind.

When I was inside my book cafe, carrying my dairy parcel from Chaturvedi Ajoba who kept insisting I call him if I need any help today, the warmth of the kitchen wrapped around me. I went ahead with the usual preparation, leaving my pets in the living room to get along with their day.

"Avni?" a familiar voice came from the front door. The voice was one but the footsteps seemed many. I wiped my hands clean and went outside to greet Chaturvedi Ajoba. As I sensed, he was not alone. Chaturvedi Ajji, Doctor Kaka, Mahima Kaki, Sudhir Kaka, Geeta Kaki from Aai's book club, and Vihaan followed him into the cafe.

"Good morning," I smiled at all of them. "How are you all today?"

"Very good. We'll be better if you brew some tea for us," Doctor Kaka said. They all pulled some chairs around and settled for breakfast.

"Sure," I replied. "What would you like to eat?" The question was directed to all of them, but only Chaturvedi Ajoba replied, "We are here to try something you youngsters eat. Right?"

The entire crew nodded and started scanning the menu card. I flipped to the clean page of my notepad and clicked the pen to write as they ordered a bunch of things.

Spinach mushroom Omelette, Club Sandwiches, and Scrambled eggs with ginger tea. And when I offered to make macaroni salad as well, they all seemed very excited to try something new.

"Okay. I'll be right back," I said and turned to walk into the kitchen. As I pulled over my apron, I heard Chaturvedi Ajoba saying, "Go help her, won't you?"

Moments later, Vihaan followed me into the kitchen.

"Hey." He hovered near the kitchen door. "How can I help?"

I wanted my beautiful big family to have one of the best mornings of all time. So I gathered all the ingredients on the counter and turned to Vihaan. "Alright. Can you slice vegetables?"

"I guess so," he replied, rather unsure.

"Get started then. Slice tomatoes, Onions, and cucumber for sandwiches. I'll dice vegetables for macaroni salad. Here's the knife and grab that chopping board," I pointed to the rack where my absolute favorite chopping boards were standing.

Once he had everything in handy, I explained to him how thick I wanted the slices to be and moved towards dicing onions, spring onion, tomato, carrot, mushroom, and bell pepper. Spinach was already washed and stored in the container. I kept it next to mushrooms and began cooking. First, I mixed some mayonnaise and yogurt with salt and black pepper. I added boiled macaroni and vegetables to the Mayonnaise and mixed it well. Garnishing with parsley and mint leaves, the salad was ready. It was colorful and creamy, just the way I wanted.

"Wow," Vihaan exclaimed, wiping his eyes with tissue paper after slicing the onion. "That looks great."

"Thank you," I blushed and started preparing scrambled eggs and Spinach Mushroom Omelette.

Once the eggs were done, I assembled the sandwiches using ingredients sliced by my assistant and poured chai into a red flowery ceramic pot and matching cups.

With Vihaan's help, I managed to serve the breakfast feast on the table within 20 minutes while my guest chatted and enjoyed their morning hours.

"Enjoy the breakfast." I placed everything on the table and kept spoons, water, and a box of tissue paper on their table.

Vihaan sat among them, biting into a sandwich and sipping tea. I watched as his eyes reflected his feeling for the chai. Our eyes met for a flicker of a second and I could feel my cheeks turning pink

"So Avni," Ajji looked at me. "How did he do in the kitchen?"

How long was she looking at me? Probably long enough to notice me staring at her grandson. *Careful, Avni.*

"Not bad," I said. "A little sloppy with the knife, but has potential to learn."

She laughed heartily as she ate a spoon full of macaroni salad. I sneaked a peek at Vihaan and found his lips curled into a small smile. I looked away before anyone else caught me looking at him and sat between Mahima Kaki and Chaturvedi Ajji so that I wouldn't be facing him. Pouring some more tea into their cups, I grabbed one for myself.

"Why aren't you eating anything?" Geeta Kaki asked. "Get yourself a plate too. Have breakfast with us, won't you?"

I nodded. Before I could serve myself, Chaturvedi Ajji grabbed a plate from the stack and served me a sandwich with salad on the side.

"Here," she said with so much affection. Chaturvedi Ajji doesn't let anyone stay hungry around her. Even if you are full, she makes you eat something. At least a Laddu.

I bit into the sandwich and felt good about it. Even though it was made by me, it felt like Chaturvedi Ajji made it with her own lovely hands.

"This is nice," Ajji said, pointing at the macaroni salad.

"Thank you Ajji. I'll give you my recipe," I smiled at her. We all enjoyed breakfast together, forgetting about the world outside that door.

"Hm," Doctor Kaka said, "This salad seems good. I think I'll try it again."

"I have more. I can pack some for you Doctor Kaka," I offered.

"I'd like that," he nodded with a smile.

Everybody loved the breakfast. "We ate too much," Sudhir Kaka declared, rubbing his hand on his belly.

"Me too," Chaturvedi Ajoba chimed in. "But worth it," he smiled at me affectionately.

The environment in the cafe was so cozy because of these people, I didn't want them to leave.

"I'll pay the bill," Sudhir Kaka walked to the counter.

"No. I believe I agreed it's my treat," Chaturvedi Ajoba declared, pulling out his wallet.

"Ajoba," Vihaan put his hand on Ajoba's arm. "I'll pay. It's my moving to Pune party."

Chaturvedi Ajoba tried to resist, but Vihaan was firm. He wouldn't let anyone else pay when he was there.

"Okay. Fine." Ajoba eventually agreed. Vihaan and I saw the group off from the door. They hovered outside the café for another 5 minutes in the name of saying 'bye' and went in their separate ways.

"It was nice to have you all here," I said while swiping his card into the machine. "It was fun."

He leaned against the counter. "They were planning it for a long while. Then Ajji said, it'll be nice to give you company today since you are alone."

"That's so nice of her." I looked towards the dairy where Chaturvedi Ajoba and Ajji were talking to customers.

I returned Vihaan's card with a bill. "Thank you," I smiled at him. He put the card back in his wallet and settled back on the sofa.

Confused, I stared at him.

"What?" he asked, pulling his laptop out of his bag which I didn't notice earlier.

"Are you...um...staying?" I hesitated. I didn't want to offend him.

"Oh, I forgot to tell you. Ajji asked me to give you company until your family returns. So I guess I'll be here." He looked over at his grandparents at the dairy and chuckled. "She said, and I quote, 'Any way you sit on the chair all day long staring into that computer of yours, might as well do it from the cafe so Avni won't be alone.'"

"She said that?" I laughed.

"Yes. She doesn't understand the concept of working from home. And I do have to go to the office once a week... which collectively makes her wonder if my job is legitimate. So, now I'm your assistant, cashier, server, whoever you want me to be. I'll be working from here."

The thought of having him with me for the entire day suddenly lifted all the tension from my shoulders. I started feeling light as a feather. How can a presence of a certain person make you feel so relaxed? I couldn't believe the effect he had on me. It all felt so new.

"Would you like to have another cup of tea?" I asked.

"Yes please," he replied, pulling the table closer to him to keep his laptop and notepad.

"I'll be right back."

I brought freshly brewed tea for both of us and sat on the sofa next to him.

"So?" I asked, shifting into my seat to face him. "How's the new job? Do you like it here?"

He sipped tea and thoughtfully replied, "Good, I guess."

"Just good?"

"Yeah." He leaned back on the sofa. "I mean, this is my first job. I was a freelancer for two years, so I'm still getting used to the work environment. This job is just temporary though."

Temporary? Does that mean he won't be here for a longer time? That makes sense. He grew up changing cities. Maybe he will go somewhere else to find a better job. Maybe staying in one place doesn't fascinate him. Pune is good though. I don't know why he won't like it here. It's perfect. He has a family here. He can work from home and spend time with his grandparents.

At that moment, for a little amount of time, I imagined my life without him in it. And I didn't like it. I know we haven't spent that much time together for me to think so ahead of time. But it's not about the time. Some people stamp their impact the moment you meet them. Vihaan is one of those people.

Right when I started picturing him not being here, he cleared his throat and said, "I've been working on something of my own. It's an app, but I haven't gotten any further."

"Really?" I replied all excited. "That's so cool. Can I see it?"

"It's not ready to show anything to you. But yes, I have been working on it for the past 2 years. It's sort of a personal finance management app. And when I launch it, it'll be as a side income for a few years until I work full-time on it."

"That's a great plan," I perked up. "I'm sure you can do it."

He chuckled at my excitement. "Yeah. The job is good, but I'd rather work on my own app. I had almost given up on it, but now I'm going to work on it every day to launch it sooner."

"Good for you," I rested my hand on his shoulder. "You'll be grateful for whatever made you change your mind. Don't give up, okay?"

He turned to look at my hand on his shoulder and his eyes traveled upon mine just for a moment. My cheeks flushed. I removed my hand from his shoulder and sat there in silence. He smiled and shifted his focus on the computer screen and typed things that I would never understand. Lines and lines of code. He looked 10 times more handsome when he was intensely coding on his laptop, eyes shining from the glow of the screen.

"I'll leave you to work." I got up and went into the kitchen to rinse our tea cups.

When he arrived in Pune, I didn't consider he might leave eventually. That possibility never crossed my mind. Now that it did cross my mind, I'm hoping from the bottom of my heart, that he would stay here. I just haven't figured out why it's so important to me.

ELEVEN

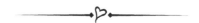

"Hey Avni, How are you?" Shweta beamed at me as she and her group entered the café. I arranged the last mystery book from the 'Sister's Crime' trope on the shelf and stood up to greet them.

"I'm good. How have you been? Glad to see you all here." I smiled at the group of six people curiously scanning the interior of the café and exchanging appreciative glances with each other. They all seemed to be in their late twenties or early thirties and were wearing casual work outfits with laptop bags hanging from their shoulders.

"Well," she said, "as promised, I have brought my whole group. Let me introduce you to everyone."

"Sure," I replied. "Why don't you take a seat?"

They all decided to sit by the window that overlooks the garden. I let them settle before offering water and a menu card.

"We are all a bunch of freelance Health and Fitness bloggers. You've already met me and Megha," Shweta began. "This is Shri, short for Raghav Shrivastav. You could say he is our boss, but we don't bother with that."

Shri laughed heartily. I shook his hand. "Welcome, Sir."

"Please call me Shri. Nobody calls me sir."

"Okay," I shyly replied. Shweta continued to her left. "This is Arnav, our editor. Ashwin, he organizes interviews with fitness experts and gym trainers to plan website content. This right here," she pointed at the guy next to Ashwin, "our photographer and graphic designer Vaibhav, and to his left is Riya, she writes about diet but I doubt she follows one herself."

I smiled and nodded at all of them.

"Megha, Riya, and I are writers. Shri manages our clients and finalizes all new articles to go live. We also have a guest blogging platform where others can share their fitness stories."

I listened as Shweta explained their work. She's a talkative and jolly person. I already liked her.

"And now," Shweta concluded her long introductory speech, "We want to know all about your work-from-café nook."

"Of course." I cleared my throat and said, "The nook is very new. In fact, you are the first group to sign up for it. You can sit wherever you like and order anything from the menu. There will be minimal table booking charges. Why don't you all give it a trial run today and we can plan it better for you?"

"That sounds great," Shri chimed in. "And what are the timings?"

"I open café at around 8:30 in the morning every day and closing time is around 9:30 PM. So you can visit anytime throughout the day. You can even call beforehand to book a particular table and order food before you arrive. I can keep everything ready."

"Perfect," Riya beamed, scanning the menu with enthusiasm.

"So we can barge in anytime?" Shri asked.

"Yes," I smiled. "Anytime."

He turned to his group, "We should ditch our co-working space. The rent is high and the food sucks."

"Agreed," Shweta added, giving me a bright smile.

"Alright. Let's order something and get some work done," Shri snatched the menu card from Riya's hand and began browsing it.

"Hey!" She frowned, but happily placed an order with her group.

I noted down everything with their preferred instructions.

· 4 Amrutatulya Chai. 2 Black Coffees. Less sugar
· 3 Corn & Cheese Sandwiches and 3 Bombay masala
· 3 plates of Mini Samosas

"That'll be all for now," Shri said. "Unless Riya has any follow-up orders."

She rolled her eyes, "mind your business Shri," and looked at me. "I'd like to try Crispy veg Cutlets too, please."

"Certainly," I scribbled it on the notepad. "Anything else?"

"That'll be all," She declared, before powering on her laptop.

"Chai and coffee on the house, since you are visiting for the first time for the nook," I offered and witnessed an amazing smile on everyone's faces.

Vihaan, who was patiently watching the whole thing from the counter, got up to help me.

"And who's this gentleman?" Shri asked as he saw Vihaan walking towards me.

"I'm Vihaan," he extended his hand to shake Shri's. "I recently moved here for my job. And you could say I work here part-time."

"Is that so? And what do you do otherwise?"

"I'm a software developer. I mostly work from home. These days from this café."

"That's awesome," Shri said. "Nice to meet you."

"Likewise, Shri." Vihaan beamed confidently. "We'll get your order soon."

"No rush," Shri smiled and shifted his focus back to his laptop.

Vihaan is very confident when he talks to people. He knows what to say and how much to tell. I wish I had that quality. I have been known to say stupid things and blurt out more than necessary information. I hope I said all the right things to Shweta's group and they will consider signing up for the nook. For that, the trial must go well.

With that thought, Vihaan and I made our way into the kitchen. I pulled over my apron and brought bread, vegetables, Samosa stuffing, and Veg cutlet mix to the kitchen counter in front of me.

"Okay." I drew a deep breath. "Let's get started."

Vihaan was pretty smooth in the kitchen this time. As I prepared sandwiches, he grilled them in my toaster. When I was frying mini samosas and cutlets, he poured tea into a teapot and placed cups on the tray. I quickly plated all the dishes with ketchup and chutney, and was ready to serve.

"Everything looks incredible, Avni," Vihaan beamed. "I think I'm hungry."

I giggled. "I've saved Samosas and cutlets. We can eat it later."

He gave me a smile that was almost like a child's smile when offered ice cream. A tiny blush stretched over my cheeks and earlobes. I quickly grabbed one of the trays before he could see my blushing face. "Let's serve this."

"Yes Ma'am!" He grabbed the second tray and followed me outside where Shweta's group was busy discussing work, glancing between each other's laptop screens.

"Here," I said, keeping the tray on the table. "Enjoy your meal."

Riya was the first to dig in, followed by the rest of the group. All of them abandoned their work as they saw food in front of them.

"Call me if you need anything." I refilled water into their glasses, kept a box of tissues on their table, and joined Vihaan by the counter.

"They're having fun," he said, watching the group as they ate, laughed, and high-fived each other with their internal jokes.

"I know right? If this all works out, I can plan these nooks in a much better way."

"I'm sure you can," he smiled at me. I don't know when I started craving Vihaan's compliments. Every time he says something nice, I feel so good about myself. The way he says it with confidence as if I can do anything. I don't feel the same about myself, but he does. And that could be the reason I like hearing him compliment me.

"I guess I'll get back to work," he said after a moment.

"Sure. Thanks for helping me. I'll check on my pets. Call me if you need me," I replied and left him to work. As much as I wanted to stay with him and talk about absolutely anything, he had his own work to finish. I didn't want to bother him. So I slipped outside to fetch my pets.

They saw me emerging from the doorway and hurried to play with me. I removed my shoes to let my ankles breathe and sat down on the patio steps. "Come here, you all." I pulled all my pets closer and hugged them. If anyone sees us right now, no one would be able to spot me. They consumed me entirely, I could hardly breathe. But I didn't mind. I love it when they are so clingy.

"You all have been such good kids today," I ruffled their fur. Harvey woofed. *Mention not, hooman.*

"Up for a treat?" I asked and the moment those words left my mouth, they started jumping around me. I managed to get up and walk past them to the cabinet where I keep dog food and snacks. My pets aren't picky. They eat chapatis, oats, biscuits, bread, and everything. I, of course, am careful with their diet. But they seem to enjoy anything I have to offer.

I grabbed their usual bowls and filled them with snacks. I sat down on the soft grass, cross-legged, and watched as my pets started filling their tummies. Seeing them so delighted with the food, I giggled under my breath. No matter what's going on in my life, these four angels always make me smile.

My phone lying next to me on the grass started buzzing with an incoming phone call. About time, I thought, when Aai's name flashed on the screen.

I answered the call and asked, "Aai. Did you all reach well?"

"We did, Avu. Don't worry," Aai's soft voice landed in my ears. "How are you? All good?"

"So far, yes," I replied.

She chuckled.

"How are Vahini's parents? Everything okay there? And Nidhi? She alright?"

"Nidhi still hasn't understood why you couldn't be here. But she is playing outside with neighborhood kids, all giggly," Aai told me.

"And Vahini's parents?"

"They are alright. But the thing is Avu, Tanvi's father hasn't been well. His knee hurts all the time and doctors have detected diabetes. So he's going to need proper treatment and diet."

I hummed in response and waited for her to continue.

"So, we are meeting another doctor in a couple of hours, just to get a second opinion."

"Is there any problem, Aai?" Concern filled my heart.

"Not really," she continued. "But they might be needing financial help. Vahini's mother is taking care of everything. But her father's pension won't be enough. Her parents didn't directly ask for help. They just wanted to see familiar faces. But it's our responsibility to help them."

"Of course, Aai. Let me know how can I help?"

"You take care of yourself, Avu. We will be back soon. I will keep you posted."

"Don't worry about me, Aai. I'm doing well. Call me as often as you can."

"I will," she replied, promising to stay in touch to figure out how we can help Vahini's parents. While Vahini visits them at least thrice every year, they might need her with them more often. And I know Vahini's heart lives here, at the store with Harsh Dada. If her parents are okay to move to Pune, temporarily if not permanent, both Vahini and I can look after them. Also, a bit of change would be good for them.

When Aai hung up our phone call, I realized that both of them might need more money with them. My mother always makes sure that I and Vahini have enough money in our bank accounts for ourselves. She doesn't know how to transfer money online, but she knows how to take care of us. And this time, I thought I'll do it for her. So I transferred some money from the book cafe's bank account to Vahini's and Aai's accounts.

My beloved Vahini doesn't ask for anything. She says she is happy with whatever she has right now. Her daughter, her family, and the books. She doesn't have to ask though. She can have everything here, it belongs to her too. She doesn't share her feelings much too. I'm sure there's a lot in her heart, buried and locked safely in the corner. Her parents keep bringing up the topic of her moving in with them for good. But she says, if Harsh was here, I would have been here. And Harsh is still here, so how could I leave?

She doesn't have to leave. And even if she one day decides to leave, I won't let her go. There was a time when Vahini and I used to go to the movies a lot. But then everything changed and all of us started thinking twice before spending money.

It will change, soon. I will change it.

My phone chimed and I found Vahini's message popping up. The phone screen was filled with happiness as I opened it to find a picture of Nidhi playing on the swing with her new friends. My niece looked so adorable that I wanted to jump into the screen to hug her. I sent back my selfie, angling the camera to capture all the four pets in the background having their meal.

"I miss you, Avu Attu," came the reply.

"I miss you more, Nidhi baby." I typed back and watched as my pets looked at me for more snacks. I filled their bowls and brushed my fingers over their forehead. I must have spent half an hour outside, thinking how I can make everyone's life comfortable. I wish I had Hermione's wand.

"Avni." Vihaan's voice came from the doorway. "The guests are leaving, could you come inside?"

"Oh of course." Giving a quick peck to all my lovely dogs, I followed Vihaan to the counter.

"I hope you had a good time," I said to my guests.

"Yes indeed. It was much much better than our co-working space. We are thinking to do this more often. Every day, rather."

"I'm happy to host you all," I smiled.

Megha was scanning the bookshelves. She joined the conversation by saying, "This place is amazing," and kept three books on the counter. "I'd like to buy these."

"I'll pack it for you," Vihaan offered and handled the bill while I talked to Shweta.

"We are thinking to book the table for three to four hours every afternoon, say 2 to 5 or something. Would that be okay?"

"Certainly. Is there anything else you might need? Wifi or extra charging points? I do have an extension that you can use."

"That'd be helpful," said Arnav. "And tea on arrival would be fantastic."

"That I can guarantee," I replied. "And if you are interested in booking the nook for an entire month, I am offering 10% off on booking charges."

"Done Deal," Shweta said. "This is my business card. Please share booking and payment details."

"Will do," I smiled at her.

"Food was amazing by the way," Shri chimed in.

"Thank you." I opened the drawer and took out a brochure of my catering portfolio. "I take catering orders too, for small or medium-sized events."

"That is fantastic." Shri took the brochure from me and read it. "We do have an upcoming meeting with clients at my home, so I'll give you a call for catering."

"Great. Thank you," I beamed. "The cake shop next door has amazing party cakes. We both do home deliveries."

"Perfect," Shweta said. "We'll see you soon. Do send nook booking details."

The group bid goodbye, leaving me overwhelmed and extremely happy.

"I can't believe my Instagram post about nooks worked out so nicely," I said to Vihaan, keeping Shweta's business card in the drawer of the counter.

He stood up and walked towards me with his hands in the pocket of his jeans, all tall and handsome. The hem of his shirt was free and loose over his jeans. He looked extra cute.

"Congratulations Boss," he said with a smile.

"Thanks." I grinned, struggling to hide the bright scarlet patches on my cheeks.

I felt so happy after a long time that I was tempted to hold Vihaan's hand and twirl around the café. How nice it would be to have nothing to worry about.

With a few catering gigs and these nooks, I'll at least have some savings in my account. I'll try to convince Madhav Kaka to extend the deadline or allow me to pay him back with installments that I can afford. If I plan everything wisely, things won't be as scary as they seem right now. And then, there will be a day when my family will have nothing to worry about.

TWELVE

As the sun slowly dipped below the horizon, a gentle blend of purple and orange spread across the sky. Nupur and I returned from delivering the cake and food to her friend's house for the graduation party. They had ordered Pav Bhaji, Samosas, and Cold Coffee for 20 people and I was able to prepare it all in my café's kitchen. Packing everything in containers, Nupur and I delivered the cakes and the food on time.

"How did it go?" Rutu asked as we sat in the garden sipping tea. Vihaan was seated on the patio chair, attending yet another virtual meeting. He turns into a complete professional mode when he's on an office call and I gotta say, I like listening to him. He sensed my gaze and looked above the laptop screen to smile at me. I smiled back and shifted my focus to my friends.

"Fantastic as usual," Nupur replied, beaming ear to ear.

Rutu took a long sip of her tea and narrowed her eyes at me.

"What?" I asked, tucking my legs beneath me to sit cross-legged.

"What's going on?" She glanced at Vihaan from the corner of her eyes.

"Nothing's going on," I replied, avoiding her eye contact. "Why do you ask?"

"Something is obviously going on."

I knew it wouldn't be practical to hide my feelings from them. Sooner or later, both of them would have figured it out anyway. It's not like my face is a good liar, in fact, my face says it all. I'll be horrified if Vihaan sensed it too.

"Do you like him?" Nupur squealed in excitement.

I shushed her, "Don't say it out loud."

"He is not going to hear us." Rutu rolled her eyes. "Now spill."

I tried my best to divert the topic to our catering event. But they wouldn't let it go. Eventually, I sighed and confessed that yes, I do have a crush on him, which has started to feel like more than a crush with each passing day.

"He's nice," I told them. "I don't know if he likes me the same way though."

"I say he does," Nupur said with a matter-of-fact tone. "Otherwise why would he spend a whole day with you here?"

"Because his Ajji told him to accompany me," I informed, defending Vihaan but also hoping Nupur's statement to be true.

"Sure," Rutu prompted, keeping her empty cup on the tray. "But now it seems like he has more than one reason to be here."

I couldn't help but smile. The thought of him liking me back warmed the center of my heart.

"I knew something was going on with you. You are smiling more than usual, which is great." Rutu perked up. "I'm really glad to see you so happy after a while."

I smiled and whispered, "I know. I kind of like having him here."

Nupur reached out to squeeze my hand. "We're happy for you, Avni."

It's been years since I smiled like this, from the heart. I never knew a genuine smile takes so much effort when you grow up. Happiness comes with a price and takes a lot to stay for a long time. I want to be able to smile like this. I want everyone around me to glow with a smile.

We girls enjoyed our evening tea and talked about so many things in one conversation. Turns out, they knew Vihaan and I'd hit it off. They saw it coming when he walked into my café the very first day and later I told them how I didn't recognize him. Nupur clapped in excitement, "It's like your fairy tale rom-com books, right? Love at first sight and everything cute." She was right. I liked the thought of living a love story that I often read in books.

"Anyway," Nupur said, getting up and brushing dust from the back of her dress. "We should get back to work." She winked at Rutu and said, "Let's leave them alone."

I rolled my eyes, "Nothing's going to happen. Don't get your hopes up."

"I already hear wedding bells," Rutu sang and got up to leave. My best friends are very dramatic. I knew this will happen, they won't stop teasing.

Both of them giggled and hugged my pets before getting back to their shops. I was glad they didn't say anything to Vihaan. His meeting was still going on when I sat across from him with my diary to check and update my agenda. Catering delivery went well, I ticked it off of the list. I had to send an email to Shweta about the Nook booking and payment package details. I powered on my laptop and sent a quick email to her. While I was at it, I scheduled a couple of pictures on social media and re-shared an Instagram story about each nook. I need to keep promoting it to get a better response. So far, only one writer has inquired about the Writer's Nook. I replied to the girl with an invitation to visit the café anytime.

"Okay. Thanks. Have a good day," Vihaan said to his teammates and hung up the meeting call. He kept his headphones dangling around his neck and stretched his arms. When I looked at him, he asked, "What are you up to?"

"Just sending some emails," I replied, hitting the send button and ticking it off of the agenda. Vihaan leaned forward and read my to-do list. When he realized what he was doing, he leaned back and said, "Sorry I didn't mean to read it."

"That's okay." I smiled at him and sent another email responding to a new inquiry.

"You wanna start a website?" He pointed at my agenda.

"Yeah," I replied and kept my laptop aside. "I do have a few ideas for the website. Online order and booking. A book club and things like that."

"You should do it," he said, suddenly all excited.

"I want to. But I don't know how much it'll cost. I'm sort of on a tight budget, so."

"It won't cost much. And I can design the whole website for you. I have done it when I was freelancing."

That was a generous offer. But I didn't say anything at the moment. I wanted to know how much it'll actually cost. Besides, designing a website sounds like a big deal. It must be time-consuming. He's already helping out in the café when he has his own work to finish. I wouldn't want to trouble him. And, the money I'm saving isn't enough right now. It won't be ideal if I spend a chunk of it on a website that can wait another couple of months.

"What's wrong?" he asked, his eyebrows knitted at the center of his temple.

"Nothing," I quickly replied. "It's just that. I don't want to overspend on the website. It's not on priority."

"Avni," Vihaan continued. "It's not that complicated. I can get it done before you know it."

I considered it for a moment, only because he was so genuinely interested to design the website. I know I can do so much with it. I have ideas scribbled everywhere in my diary. But I can't take favor from him. He's already helping me more than needed.

I nervously interlocked my fingers in my lap and asked, "How much will it cost?"

"Um..that depends on the hosting plan we select. But I'm sure I can get a cheaper deal through my friend's affiliate."

"Can you give me an estimate?"

He unlocked his phone and searched for something before saying, "If you want to list books to sell, you'll need an e-commerce extension on your website." He turned his phone screen towards me to show me the estimated cost. It was decent but not ideal at the moment. Still, I considered it, wondering if it might help in expanding book sales.

"And what do I owe you...you know...for creating the entire website?"

Vihaan's eyes drifted from his phone and landed straight on my eyes, "What?"

I didn't repeat it. I know he heard it and it already took all of my courage to ask him that.

"You can't possibly think I'll take money from you, Avni."

"And you can't possibly think I'll let you do it for free. You are already doing a lot. You have your own job to work for. I know the website won't be an easy task and I can't ask you to do it for free," I replied, matching his tone. "There's a lot I still have to figure out."

He opened his mouth to say something but didn't. I stayed quiet too. What else there was to say? The conversation ended as if it never started in the first place. I could see his face shifting expressions. Offending him in any way was not at all in my mind.

"Look Vihaan." I kept my tone as gentle as possible. "There's no way I'm comfortable letting you do it for free. And now is not a good time for me to invest money in a website. Maybe a couple of months later."

"Alright. Whatever you want." That was all he could say. I wanted him to say something else. Anything. But he didn't. His silence made me uncomfortable. Is he mad at me? I didn't mean to hurt his feelings. I felt terrible. Uncomfortable silence hovered between us. I wanted to say sorry but the buzzing of his phone interrupted my thoughts.

He answered the phone and said, "Yeah. I'll be there in a moment."

"Avni," he met my eyes. "I need to go home."

I watched him pack his laptop bag and swing it on his shoulder. He pocketed his phone, got up from the seat and said, "I'll be back soon."

"Okay," I whispered, still trying to figure out his reaction. He turned around and walked inside the café through the patio doorway. I followed him inside, matching my pace with his. I wanted to say, *Stay. Don't go.* But couldn't. He opened the main door and walked across the road to his apartment building without taking one last glance at me. I stood by the window, waiting for him to turn around and look at me. My heart sank when he didn't turn once.

Feeling guilty for refusing his help, I slumped on the sofa and wrapped my arms around myself. My pets emerged from the patio doorway and settled in the Reader's Corner to feel warm and cozy. Apart from them and me, there was not a single soul around me. No guests, no friends, no family chatter, *no Vihaan*.

The loneliness started eating me. I wanted to scream inside the pillow. Instead, as any sane person would do, I put on light music in the background. John Legend's *All Of Me* filled the atmosphere. I closed my eyes to take a moment to myself. I wanted to gather all my thoughts in a big bowl and sort them one by one in tiny containers. So I can keep the good ones to myself and throw the bad ones down the drain.

Baba. I miss my Baba. I wish I could talk to him, maybe through his diary. I was completely aware that the last entries in his diary would break me. But I wanted to read the last thoughts he ever wrote.

I leafed through pages after pages of updates about his work-in-progress book. If back then somebody had told me that would be my Baba's last book, I would never have believed it. But life is unpredictable.

Glancing at my life through his eyes was both beautiful and painful. He thought about his family every time he picked up his pen to write in his diary. Not a single page was all about him. It was always about somebody else. Mostly his children and granddaughter.

I came across a page where he wrote- *Next year, Avni will graduate. When did she grow up so much? Feels like yesterday when I dropped her at school, holding her tiny hand. Now she'll soon be old enough to start her own business. As much as I love seeing my children grow, I miss their childhood. I miss them running in the house with nothing to worry about. I hope their lives will be always happy and adventurous.*

A tiny drop of tear landed on the page, scattering the ink. I closed the diary before I ruin Baba's handwriting with my tears. He wanted to do so many things but couldn't. It saddened my heart, bringing back the memory of the day he and Dada waved at us from the doorway. They were going to attend a literary event to meet authors. The last thing I said to Baba and Dada was – 'Bring me signed copies from the event, as many as you can get.' Baba had laughed and said, 'Why do you think I'm carrying such a big bag?' I never heard his laugh again. Dada had pulled my ponytail before leaving. "See you soon," he had said.

I brought my knees to my chest and hugged myself. Teardrops started escaping my eyelids. I felt lonelier than ever. A mere thought of what would happen if I fail to return Madhav Kaka's money twisted my stomach in a knot.

My heart started pounding with fear of the unknown. Fear of what lies ahead. I frantically scanned the surroundings to find a familiar face. Baba? Harsh Dada? Aai? Vahini? But there were none. I stayed seated hopelessly, wondering what to do with Madhav Kaka. Why was he doing this? What good it would do to anyone? More tears rolled down my cheeks as I imagined losing my Baba's business to someone who wouldn't care about it. He will probably sell it and that thought broke my heart into pieces. I closed my eyes and rested my head on my knees. I don't know how long I was sitting in the same spot. Probably an hour? I couldn't tell.

I heard footsteps approaching as the doorbell chimed. Assuming it must be a customer, I immediately wiped my eyes and stood up to greet them.

"Avni?" Vihaan's voice reached straight to my heart. "What happened? Why are you…"

I didn't let him finish. I ran towards him and wrapped my arms around his neck as tightly as he could take.

Sobbing, I buried my face between his jaw and shoulder blade, inhaling his presence. He smelled like...home.

A moment later, I felt his arms wrapping around my waist. He held me tightly with one arm and tangled his other hand in my curls, holding me closer.

"Hey," he softly whispered. "What's wrong?"

I snuggled even closer to him and replied, "I'm sorry. I just felt...I don't know... scared."

"It's okay. I'm here." He slowly leaned behind to look at me. "Don't worry."

I unwrapped myself from him. A strand of my hair remained hovering on his cheek. He was too close to me, so close that I could feel his warm breath on my face.

He let go of my waist and I stepped slightly away from him to gather my feelings. He waited for me to say something. Wiping my face, I sat down on the sofa. Vihaan sat beside me and wrapped his arm around my shoulder to hold me close to him.

"What's wrong?" he asked again. His tone was softer than before.

I didn't want to burden him with my problems. I'd rather not talk about it altogether.

"I felt lonely," I replied with a tight throat.

"You are not," he said.

"Are you mad at me? For earlier?" I asked, wiping my nose.

"What? No. Ajji wanted my help, that's all." He rubbed my shoulder to comfort me. "Don't worry about anything. I'm right here."

His words made me look him in the eyes. This time, I didn't look away. His eyes were calm and caring. Those shiny brown eyes assured me I won't be alone. I could feel myself losing into them, captivated by the depth. He held my gaze, reaching straight to my heart, and said, "You know you can tell me anything, right? If something's bothering you…"

"Yeah." I dabbed tissue paper on my cheeks. "I know. Thank you."

"Now smile. A big one." He leaned back and looked at my face. "Come on."

I flashed all my teeth at him and grinned widely.

"That's better," he said with a smile.

I chuckled and gathered myself. Vihaan stayed with me for a long time, until closing time, to make sure I was okay, to make sure I wasn't alone anymore.

THIRTEEN

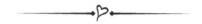

Sometimes, a good cry and a long night's sleep can make you feel better. I didn't hold back my tears, and neither did I deny my fears. Burying it deep will only make it difficult for me. I allowed myself to recall memories and overthink things that I always run away from. I cried until there was not a single drop of tear left in my eyes and fell asleep listening to an audiobook. When I woke up, the morning sunshine poured through the window and wrapped a sense of calm around me.

I sat up on my bed and checked my phone. 2 messages from Aai telling me Vahini's father is okay and that she'll call me later. One message from Vahini asking if I was okay. And three missed calls from Chaturvedi Ajji. When I called her back, she invited me for breakfast. "Rutu and Nupur are joining too. Stop by at 8," she said in her lovely grandmother's voice.

Vihaan must have told her that I wasn't feeling well. I don't know how much he told her about last evening, but I was glad about the invitation. It's not the first time Ajji has invited people for breakfast. Today could be just one of them. Either way, I felt really good as I walked to Rhythm Lane.

By the time I reached, Rutu and Nupur were already waiting for me in the passageway. My dogs jumped in delight as Sudhir Kaka offered them loads of snacks. Leaving them to it, we girls made our way to Vihaan's apartment.

Chaturvedi Ajoba opened the door with his usual cheerful smile. "Welcome, welcome." He stepped aside to let us through. We went inside and a delicious aroma of Rava Upma and Thalipeeth filled our nostrils. *Total Bliss.*

"Smells heaven in here," I said to Chaturvedi Ajji. "Do you need any help in the kitchen?"

"No no. It's almost done. You girls can sit on the balcony if you want. I'll be right out."

Ajoba handed me a rug that I spread on the balcony. We all sat down enjoying the morning breeze and watching Rhythm Lane. Ajoba told us about his recent adventures. Apparently, Rhythm Lane senior citizen group went to play cricket at the stadium against the senior citizen team from a nearby neighborhood. We laughed as he animatedly described his experience.

I was listening to him but my eyes were constantly scanning the surroundings to find Vihaan, who hadn't made an appearance yet. My thoughts wandered to our last evening's hug, flooding my mind with gentle memories.

"Looking for someone?" Chaturvedi Ajoba asked and my heart skipped a beat. Oh god. Am I making it too obvious? In that case, everyone will figure it out, even Vihaan, and I'll end up embarrassing myself.

"Just my pets," I replied, quickly gathering my thoughts and changing the subject. "You didn't open the dairy today, Ajoba?"

"Oh, I did open it in the morning. But wife called to take a break." He shrugged with a smile. "Can't say no to her."

"Such a nice morning." Chaturvedi Ajji came out holding a tray of Rava Upma and Thalipeeth for all of us. "With my favorite girls."

"Thanks for inviting us, Ajji." Rutu helped herself with a plate of Upma sprinkled with lemon juice and coriander. We all grabbed our plates and made space for Ajji to sit with us.

"It's my pleasure, dear. Take more. I have made plenty."

Ajji is a Sugaran. Anything she makes turns into magic. I took a spoonful of Upma and as expected, it was delicious.

"It's too good, Ajji," I complimented her with a chef kiss. "Thalipeeth is amazing too."

I dipped a bite of Thalipeeth in yogurt and was about to take a bite when Vihaan came outside, wearing shorts and a vest, carrying a tray of teapot and cups in one hand, and brushing the other hand through his wet hair.

He greeted us all with a smile and looked over at me for a moment before taking a seat next to Ajoba. My silly heart exploded with butterflies. I couldn't look away from the sight in front of me. Looking away would be an insult to him. I stared at the man who I didn't know could take my breath away so easily. I lost all sense of the surroundings. I could feel my skin reddening as I watched him pour tea into cups. And I was pretty sure people around me could see it too. But I wanted to look at him for as long as nature allows me.

To my left, Nupur cleared her throat and coughed loudly to flinch me out of my dreamland. She pinched my arm and widened her eyes at me. "What are you doing?" she whispered. "Not smooth."

Rutu giggled as she watched my confused and embarrassed face. Horrified by my actions, I quickly glanced at Ajji and Ajoba. Thankfully, both of them were busy with their own conversation. I was glad they didn't notice anything. And even after all that, I couldn't resist one last glance at Vihaan. I thought I saw a slight smile on his face. I could be wrong, but I so wanted to be right.

For the next 10 minutes, we all chatted with each other. I participated in the conversation to occupy myself with anything but Vihaan's thoughts. He was right there, making me nervous by his mere presence.

Ajoba handed over tea cups to all of us and took one for himself. Tea was exactly what I needed to get rid of all the tension. I sipped it with delight.

"How are Tanvi's parents?" Ajji asked, looking at me.

"They are fine. Aai and Vahini are meeting doctors and dietitians for her father," I replied. "They might have to stay for a couple of more days."

"Tanvi should bring her parents here. They'll feel better among us."

"That's what I think," I smiled at her. "They'll love it here."

"Nidhi must be missing you," Ajoba asked, sipping tea.

I nodded, "She's being dramatic."

Ajji and Ajoba both laughed. Nidhi loves spending time with them. They tell her stories and she sometimes takes a nap at their house. "We are missing her too," Ajji said. "Everything is quiet without her."

I nodded with a smile. The morning hour unfolded beautifully as I sat there with my friends, sipping tea so divine I could melt into it. When we finished breakfast, we girls wrapped our arms around Ajji and consumed her in a hug. "Thank you Ajji. You are the best." Every time Ajji feeds us with her food garnished with love, we all feel extra energized. She hugged us back and waved at us from the door as if we were her 5-year-old granddaughters.

When I finally opened my café and walked into the kitchen, I found myself smiling. Last night, I was crying because I felt lonely and here I was, returning from a family breakfast. As long as I am surrounded by these people, I would never be alone.

With that thought, I prepared the kitchen and opened the backdoor to let my pets get on with the day. Even they were happy as Sudhir Kaka pampered them well. I offered them some water and made my way into Reader's Corner to unpack a box of books that Vahini hadn't done yet.

The box was still sealed when I pulled it over on the rug. I opened it and was immediately greeted by the fragrance of new books, the ink on the paper, and the colorful cover designs. It was a treasure of some of my favorite authors and some books that I haven't read yet. Before sorting the books, I quickly clicked a picture of the box with books, then one with books spread on the rug, and one I planned to click after I arrange them. That'll make a good *Before-After* Instagram post.

There were 3 books by Ruskin Bond, something many people grew up reading. This time, Vahini had also ordered Chacha Chaudhary. She was planning to conduct a *Good Old Memories* themed book club session with the ladies. Such a great idea.

Clubbing books by authors and then sorting them by Genre, I placed them on the shelves where they belong and clicked a picture.

"You look busy." A melodious voice came from the doorway. I turned around to find Vihaan leaning against the door frame with his arms folded on his chest. His hair, now a dry soft crown, made him look ten times more handsome.

"Not at all. Come join me."

He took a seat on the sofa and grabbed one of my favorite romance books lying on the rug. He turned it over to read the blurb on the back cover and started flipping the pages, his expression turning into curiosity.

"You like it?" I asked, sitting back on the rug.

"Not my type," he declared, still reading the blurb. "But seems interesting."

"Have it," I said, folding the empty book box and keeping it aside.

"No," he quickly replied. "I don't read these kinds of books."

"First of all, that's rude." I held his gaze. "Try it for me. We can buddy-read if you want."

"We can what now?"

I chuckled. "Buddy read. Means we can either read it together here, or you can read at your own pace and I at my own."

He took a moment to answer but it was positive. "Alright. Let's do this weird thing."

"It's not weird," I replied defensively. "It's fun. Give it a try and we can discuss it later."

"Okay cool. But only this time. Don't make it a habit."

I grinned widely. "Sure."

While I edited the picture for social media, Vihaan opened his laptop and started working. We both stayed silent and did our work. The silence was comforting and easy. It wasn't awkward at all. I think we've both gotten used to being in each other's presence. Though, we haven't brought up the topic of our *Hug* yet. I think Vihaan wants to respect my feelings and I don't want to put him in an awkward situation either. Things like these are best left where they were, to cherish them forever.

"Hey, Avni?" Vihaan called without shifting his gaze from the screen.

"Hm?" I added the hashtags and posted the pictures on Instagram.

"I know you don't want to launch your website yet, but hear me out," he turned his laptop screen so I could see it better. "It's a reasonable deal and we don't have to pay all at once. They have monthly small payment options. What do you think?"

I looked over at his screen and bit my lower lip. "I don't know," I replied rather unsure. "We need to discuss it..."

"Sure." He shifted his gaze from the screen to me. "What do you want to know?"

"First of all," I hesitated and chose my words carefully, "I am not going to let you do it for free. And you are not ready to take money from me. So I would like you to propose an alternative. What can I do for you in exchange for this?"

He rubbed his thumb on his jaw, thinking about my request. Then he smiled and said, "I have an idea."

I folded my legs and sat straight. "Go on."

"How about, I design your website and you show me around Pune? I haven't seen the popular places of Pune yet, and this would be a nice time off for you too?" He paused for a moment, then continued, "When do you usually take time off?"

I never realized that before. When do I really take a break? When were Baba and Dada used to take a break? Even though the shop used to be closed on Wednesday evenings, Baba and Dada used to stay here to organize books, hanging the closed sign on the door. Maybe I can follow the same schedule. Since the day I opened the cafe, I haven't taken a break. Maybe because I can't afford to take a break?

Vihaan was patiently waiting for my answer. I wanted to go out with him, do something for him. "Wednesday evening okay with you?"

"More than okay," he smiled.

"Great." I smiled back. "Thanks for doing this."

He hummed, half listening half working on his laptop. Seeing him here, in front of me, I realized *once again,* how much I adore him. How much I like to be with him. How much I...*love* him? The thought nearly startled me. Would he feel the same about me if I confess? Or would I end up hurting him and myself? These things are tricky. I've had crushes in schools and colleges, in fictional books too. But never have I ever felt so happy and certain about someone. It's different. Way different than what my fragile mind can handle.

"Vihaan?" I reached for the pillow from the armchair and rested it on my lap.

"Hm?" he looked over at me. His brown eyes shone with sunlight coming from the window.

Do you like me?

"Would you like to go by bus or should I borrow Nupur's scooty? For Wednesday?"

Silly me.

"Oh. Bus would be fun. Unless you want to take a scooter. I can drive Ajoba's Van too if you prefer that?"

"Nah. Bus will be fun."

"Alright." He looked at me with confusion. As if he sensed that wasn't what I wanted to ask. But he didn't say anything. *Thank god.*

I don't think I will ever be able to tell him how I feel about him. And if he doesn't feel the same, I guess I'm okay with being good friends with him, hoping one day, he will fall for me the way I am falling for him every single day.

FOURTEEN

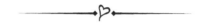

"We heard you are taking him out?" Nupur frowned as she walked towards me from her shop. I was getting interrogated outside my café by my friends whom I love so dearly.

"And we found out about it from Chaturvedi Ajji," Rutu rolled her eyes. "We thought you are our friend."

"Are you two done being dramatic?" I flipped the sign to *closed* and locked the door. "I am not taking him out. Don't make it sound like a date. I'm just showing him around because he is going to help me with the website."

"You didn't even invite us," Nupur added, ignoring my explanation.

"Do you want to join us?" I offered, genuinely.

"Naah," Nupur dropped her act way sooner than Rutu. "You go have fun. We are just messing with you."

"You can't keep up, can you?" Rutu rolled her eyes at Nupur.

"I'm so excited for her," Nupur squealed and hugged me.

"Me too," Rutu added, winking at me. "Tell us everything when you return."

"Do I have an option?"

"Not really," both of them chimed in.

I tugged at the door to confirm it was locked and shoved the keys in my bag. Rutu was fussing about me changing an outfit, but I ignored her. I was wearing a perfectly fine red tunic kurta over sky blue jeans, paired with my favorite Jutti shoes. My hair open, eyeliner symmetrical, and my lipstick just a hint of red.

"Have fun." Both of them smiled cheekily as Vihaan appeared from his apartment building, wearing a navy blue shirt over beige trousers, looking like a million bucks.

"Ready?" he asked, joining me outside my café.

"Yeah." I waved at my best friends, "See you guys later."

I was looking forward to this moment for the last couple of days. Spending time with Vihaan outside Rhythm Lane. Showing him the gems of my city. Walking through the lanes of Pune, clicking pictures together. I visualized this whole thing in my head over and over again.

I had already messaged Shweta that the café would be closed this evening. So her team spent the morning working from my café. "We'll get work done sooner," Shri prompted. When they left, I swapped my T-shirt with the Tunic I'm wearing and re-did my makeup for my 'not a date.'

Leaving my pets with Nupur, Vihaan and I walked down the lane to the bus stop. As we waited for our bus to arrive, I told him about our plan for the evening.

"Oh, here's our bus," I pointed at the approaching bus. "Let's go."

Vihaan's eyes widened as he examined the crowd inside the bus. None of the seats were empty. A lot of passengers were standing in the passage holding the hanging handles, struggling to stand in place.

"Are you sure about this? We can still take Ajoba's Van."

"Shut up," I grabbed his arm and pulled him into the bus behind me. "It'll be fine."

Reluctantly, he followed me through the crowd. I found a place for us to stand in the passage and bought two tickets.

Vihaan leaned against the handrail and folded his arms over his chest, critically scanning the bus.

"Relax," I told him. "We are getting down in less than 30 minutes."

He nodded, making some space for me to stand next to him. The bus drove through bustling Kothrud, giving us glimpses of the neighborhoods, bouncing as it crossed unnecessarily large speed breakers and stopped at the signal. Vihaan's eyes were hooked to the window, watching the passing city. I was clutching the handrail to balance myself and protecting my tote bag with my other arm. The bus really was too crowded. I should have listened to Vihaan to take Ajoba's van or we could have waited for the next bus. I could hardly stand in this one.

As the signal turned green, our bus jerked forward. A lot of people lost their balance. My hand slipped and I got pushed forward by the crowd behind me. I closed my eyes as I bumped into Vihaan in a failed attempt to balance myself.

"Easy. Are you okay?" He wrapped one arm around my waist to steady me.

I looked up to meet his gaze. He was smiling at me, holding me closer to him.

"Yeah. I'm fine." I managed to mumble under his gaze.

"Hold my arm," he offered.

I nodded and hooked my arm around his. He shifted to the side to tuck me next to him. At that moment, I realized how strong his arms were. Standing next to him, I could feel my heart racing. We were so close that I could smell his perfume. Boarding a crowded bus wasn't a bad idea after all. I kept my arm tangled with his for the rest of the journey. Around 20 minutes later, we got down from the bus in the heart of Pune city where everything is vibrant and more chaotic than the bus we just left.

Vihaan frantically looked around to capture every single thing in his eyes.

"So," I spread my arms around. "This is Pune for you."

He looked at me and then again at the city around us. When I say city, I'm not referring to huge buildings, modern cafes, shopping malls, or electric buses. I'm referring to shops that might have been here for over a hundred years. Temples that define the beauty of Pune. Indian snacks and sweets shops that export items overseas. A huge market where everything is inexpensive and beautiful. Roadside stalls curated on the back of a bicycle, selling socks, scarves, handkerchiefs, or shoes. A lane of stationery stores for wholesale school supplies. And traditional *Maharashtrian* culture.

"Where to now?" Vihaan asked, still looking around to see everything.

"Follow me."

I led him through the narrow footpath towards the temple that can take anyone's breath away. The famous, mesmerizing, complete sight to the eyes, the *Dagdusheth Ganpati* temple. People come here from all over India to make a wish because they believe it'll come true. My entire family used to come here every year during Ganesh Festival. We didn't make any wishes, but we did thank *Ganesha* for what we already have. And today, I'll be doing the same.

"This is amazing," Vihaan mumbled in surprise, following me to the entrance of the temple that's so shiny and golden, it makes the whole path lighten up.

"I'll bring you here again during the Ganesh Festival. It's way more amazing then. The five Ganesh temples, what we call *Manache Ganpati*, along with Dagdusheth Ganpati make streets go crazy. People practically live on the streets, dancing and praying, capturing pictures, and eating sweets. It's so energetic, you'd want to come every year."

"I'd love that," he said, following my suit to remove the shoes and placing them in the shoe rack outside the temple. We joined the queue and waited for it to move ahead. While I was telling Vihaan everything I knew about the temple, his eyes were wandering everywhere in the temple with awe. The queue moved ahead at a steady pace, bringing us closer to Ganesha.

Once we were inside, Vihaan's jaw dropped. Astonished at the sight, he asked, "Is it always like this?"

"Of course. It's *Shreemant Dagdusheth Temple.* Rich."

As we stood at the center of the temple, we had a perfect view of the Ganesh idol bedecked with beautiful gold jewelry. The Dagdusheth Ganpati is known for its richness. The entire *Gabhara*- the heart of the temple- is decorated with real gold and precious stones. Vihaan and I joined our palms. I thanked God for everything I have and asked for a blessing to pursue my envisioned future for the book cafe.

Before moving ahead, I took one last glance at Ganesha and gestured for Vihaan to take a seat for a couple of minutes. We sat on the temple floor watching people pray and present *Naividya* offerings to God. The temple was filled with so many people, yet it was peaceful. So peaceful that even Vihaan didn't want to go anywhere.

"Come on." I joined my palms at Ganesha before walking ahead. "We gotta go."

It took him a few minutes to actually get up and follow me outside. We got back our shoes from the rack and glanced back at the temple one more time before moving ahead.

"Where to next?" He curiously asked.

I pointed across the street. "*Tulshibaug Market.*"

We walked on the footpath to reach one of the entry points for the massive maze of a market called *Tulshibaug*. This place is always crowded. Vihaan's eyes widened when he saw the crowd in the market. He looked over at me, unsure what to do next.

"Listen," I adjusted the strap of my bag on my shoulder and shifted closer to him. "Hold hands. This is too much."

He chuckled, "Avni, I'm a grown man. Why would I get lost in a crowd?"

"Who says I'm talking about you?" I shrugged with a sheepish grin.

That made him laugh from the heart. "Okay, I'll lead the way."

I grabbed his arm and stayed as close to him as I could manage through the crowd of people bargaining, shopping, moving ahead, and bargaining some more. I've been living in Pune my whole life, yet I never trace back the same path. I get lost in the middle of the market and then come out of an entirely different exit point.

We walked past shops of clothes, shoes, cutlery, baby products, toys, books, jewelry, and repeat. If I'm guessing correctly, there are more than 300 shops squeezed like a maze in the market. People come here to buy cheaper but somewhat trendy stuff.

A small jewelry stall caught my eye on our way ahead. A girl no older than 16 was selling beautiful Zumkas, Bracelets, and delicate Anklets. I couldn't resist. My legs automatically turned to make their way through the crowd to reach the stall. Vihaan, confused by a sudden change of direction, followed me.

"How much for this?" I asked the girl, picking up a pair of Zumkas.

"30 rupees, Didi," she said with a smile. "50 for 2 pairs."

Vihaan stood behind me, protecting me from the crowd bumping into one another.

"Try it on, Didi," the girl said, holding a hand mirror in front of me. I carefully took out the Jhumkas from the packet and tried them on. When I glanced in the mirror at my reflection, Vihaan was looking straight at my ears, and then his eyes flicked at mine.

I blushed and looked down so he wouldn't catch my reddening cheeks. The girl smiled, "You look beautiful, Didi."

"I'll take it, and these too," I said pointing at small hoop earrings, keeping the Zumka earrings dangling from my ears to accessorize my curls.

"How much for this bracelet?" Vihaan leaned forward and picked up a bracelet from the collection.

"50 Rupees, Dada," the girl told him.

"We'll take it," he said, handing a 100 rupee note to the girl.

He pulled out the bracelet from the pouch, took my right hand in his, and slid the bracelet on my wrist. "Suits you," he said, smiling at me. It all happened so quickly, I didn't have a chance to react.

A massive bubble of butterflies burst into my heart. My arms, my entire body had goosebumps. I found myself losing in the moment as the world moved around us. I could feel his gaze traveling from my face to my ears to my wrist to my shoes and then, his lips curled up. I tucked my hair behind my ear and looked down at my new sparkly bracelet. I knew, if I looked up, my eyes would meet his and I would fall deep into them.

"Anything else, Didi?" the girl snapped me out into reality. When I turned to see her, she was smiling.

I managed to shake my head. Vihaan again led the way through the market. I was still processing the moment, replaying it over and over again in my heart. He bought me a gift. I would cherish these earrings and bracelet for the rest of my life. Smiling to myself, I walked closer to him, hooking my arm to his so I won't get dragged away in the crowd.

We reached the heart of the market, the very center where lots of shops were selling decorative items, fairy lights, sparkly ribbons, and cute ceramic teapot sets.

"Oh wait," I tugged at his arm. "I want to buy new teapots for the cafe."

"Okay." Vihaan followed me into the shop, keeping a close distance. I made it a quick stop and purchased a couple of fairy lights, tiny showpieces for bookshelves, and 3 sets of teapots and cups. Happy with my purchase, we moved ahead, watching a bustling lane of shops. By the time we made it to the other end of the market, it was 5 in the evening.

"Tea?" I asked Vihaan, pointing at the roadside tea stall across the street.

"Absolutely," he replied.

We crossed the road to the tea stall and ordered two cups. Standing on the sidewalk, we sipped refreshing tea and watched, by far, the most happening lane of Pune.

"This was fun," Vihaan said, running his hand through his hair.

"It's not over yet. We still have one more stop to make."

"Where?"

"Fergusson College Road," I told him as we made our way to the bus stop.

FIFTEEN

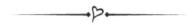

It's different when Vihaan spends time at my book cafe. But here, showing him around some of my favorite places, no one is interrupting us. Not even my own thoughts. Just me and him walking freely with hands hooked to one another, making jokes and laughing. We have never laughed so much before. I had forgotten the feeling of hurting my tummy after laughing. But as I said, I wanted the day to be memorable for both of us. So I made sure to leave all my worries at home.

After we left Tulshibaug Market, I took Vihaan to a slightly farthest bus stop, so we could see *Shaniwar Wada* palace and *Lal Mahal* palaceon our way. In both places, two of the greatest warriors of all time once lived and marked glorious history. *Shreemant Bajirao Peshwe and Chatrapati Shivaji Maharaj.* I told Vihaan the history I know of both places. We didn't go inside as it was getting late, but we did get a glimpse of both places.

When we boarded the bus to reach Fergusson College Road, aka FC road, our feet were hurting from all the walking. Luckily, the bus wasn't much crowded. Vihaan let me take the window seat as he slid next to me. Once we were settled, I checked my phone to see any message from Aai or Vahini. None so far.

My eyes drifted from the phone screen to the sparkly new bracelet on my wrist. I smiled, replaying that beautiful moment in my head. How he made me feel so special with such a simple gesture. I wanted to cherish this feeling forever, something to look at and remember the day when I wandered carefree with a man who took my breath away every time he smiled at me.

I turned to look at Vihaan who was reading some sort of article on his phone. "Hey, Vihaan?"

"Hm?"

"Selfie?" I reluctantly asked.

"Sure," he replied with a soft smile.

As I angled my phone's camera, he leaned towards me to fit into the frame. I could feel his warm breath on my neck, giving me goosebumps. It was not easy for me to keep my composure in check. But I managed to smile as normally as possible and snapped a couple of pictures.

"Send them to me too," he said, glancing at my phone screen as I scrolled through the pictures.

"Of course."

The bus took turns and brought us to the other part of the city where the FC road was blooming. Fergusson College is one of the oldest and finest colleges in Pune. And the road it stands on is another popular shopping attraction. It's similar to Tulshibaug, but not as confusing. It's a straight road, outlined with stalls of clothes, footwear, books, and food.

We got off the bus and walked by the stores for a while as I told Vihaan how Nupur, Rutu, and I used to come here quite often for shopping.

"The road adjacent to this has plenty of restaurants and roadside food stalls," I told him.

He hummed and shoved his hands in his pocket, listening to me as we walked ahead. "Where are we going exactly?" he asked, pausing to sip water from my bottle.

"Nowhere in particular," I declared. "We are just walking."

"Okay."

He followed me as I showed him some of my favorite shops, roadside chat corners, and a sandwich place where my friends and I ate chocolate sandwiches almost every time we came here. He was listening attentively as I talked, chuckling in between.

We walked until we reached the other end of the lane where a woman was selling bags. I decided to buy a cute fluffy unicorn sling bag for Nidhi and new wallets for Vahini and Aai.

On the pavement outside a tea shop, a man was singing a song over the tune of his guitar. People were stopping by to click his pictures with appreciative nods. Another man, slightly older, was painting a live picture of the surroundings. His brush swiftly filled the canvas with magic. Further ahead, a young girl was showing card tricks. And next to her, her brother was selling coloring books.

Vihaan watched everything, intrigued by the creativity. He clicked some pictures on his phone. We stood there for a while, witnessing the colorful surroundings.

"Let's go have something to eat," I pointed at the restaurant. "What would you like to have?"

"How about Misal Pav?" he asked, pocketing his phone.

I smiled and nodded. We crossed the road to the restaurant where getting a seat could be a challenge. I'd say it was great luck on our side as we were able to grab the table at the far end of the restaurant and dropped ourselves into the chairs, tired but happy.

When the waiter came to attend our table, I placed an order of two plates of medium spicy Misal Pav with extra Tarri.

"You'll love the Misal," I told him. "This is one of my favorite places to eat Misal."

He smiled and asked, "What are your favorite restaurants here?"

That was a topic of a long conversation. I sipped some water and told him my favorite restaurants, cafés, Dhabas, and what exactly I love to eat there. Where to find the best Momos in Pune and which restaurants serve the best Chinese food. Where to go when you have Biryani cravings and which chat corner serves the best Bhel Puri. He listened as I talked endlessly.

"I'll take you everywhere," I said to him.

"I'd like that," he replied with a smile.

I removed my Juttis to free my toes and sat comfortably. My shoulder was hurting from carrying an unnecessarily heavy tote bag. I gave my shoulder a slight shake and leaned against the chair.

"Why do you carry a bag as big as yourself?" he asked.

I laughed. "I have so much stuff to carry. Half of it might not be relevant, but I don't bother taking it out."

He shook his head and smiled. Around us, the fragrance of food was dancing in the air. My stomach rumbled at the thought of Misal Pav. I sipped some water to suppress the embarrassing growling noise of my tummy.

Vihaan's phone buzzed with a message. He unlocked it to read the text and beamed at me, "Your website domain has been registered. Do you have any ideas for the website?"

"I have so many ideas," I perked up.

Vihaan smiled. "Tell me what you want."

"Okay, so I was wondering if it is possible to make 'Book Box' subscriptions? I mean...I will handpick a book of the month, pair it with food items, some bookmarks, and cards, and send out monthly boxes to local subscribers. For example, if a book is a dark mystery, I would add spicy food. If it's a cute romance, maybe some cupcakes from Nupur. And then, I was also thinking I would create book boxes with 10-20 books with specific or mixed genres. Something like that."

"That's a brilliant idea," he said with an encouraging tone. "We can certainly do that."

"I was also thinking about starting a new book club. Aai and Vahini have their own, but they have different tastes in books. I was planning to start it for a long time, and Prachiti would be perfect as a host, don't you think?"

"Absolutely!"

"So can you do that on the website?"

"Of course," he answered. "I can do anything on the website. Just say a word."

"Okay great," I rubbed my palms together. "I'm really excited about it."

He chuckled, watching my overly excited face.

"Thanks for doing this," I added. "I wouldn't have been able to do it without you."

"That's not true. You definitely would have been able to do it, one way or the other. I just happen to be the lucky one."

Oh.

"I...well thanks anyway."

"Pleasure is all mine, miss," he said in a weird accent, making me giggle.

"Here's your Misal Pav." The waiter broke the chain of thoughts running in my head and served us food.

"Thank you," Vihaan said to him and looked at me. "Dig in."

We chatted about Vihaan's work as we ate our food. I asked him about his childhood and his college years, curious to know the Vihaan I didn't get to meet. He told me about his passion for coding, the projects he did during his engineering, and his favorite spy movies that he thinks I should definitely watch. When I asked him about his parents, he told me everything about them.

"Baba is thinking of retiring now, he wants to stay at one place too." Vihaan took a bite of Misal Pav and told me that he has lived in so many different places in and outside Maharashtra over the years.

"I never had a single place to call home my whole life. We were always moving cities. I had to change schools quite often."

"That must have been tough."

"At first, yes. Then I got used to it. The only constant thing in my life was my grandparents. They would visit every Diwali and summer holidays to spend time with me, wherever we were staying that year. I used to look forward to it."

"Hm...but did you like any of the cities you were living in?"

"I liked them all. But then we moved again. And the cycle kept repeating. Now when I look back, I think my comfort zone was pretty wider. It kind of boosted my confidence. But now I'm done moving."

I nodded understandingly. I can't imagine leaving Rhythm Lane, let alone Pune.

Vihaan sipped some water and continued, "Ajoba tried to convince my Baba a lot, that they would take me to Pune and keep me at one place, one school. But my parents didn't want to miss my growing up years."

I offered a soft smile and let him continue.

"Now...here I am. My job brought me to Ajoba. I was explicitly checking the job openings in Pune." He smiled, "Ajoba and Ajji were over the moon when I told them I was coming to live with them."

"I remember," I chuckled. "He was telling me the day you were supposed to arrive. He was so happy."

Vihaan nodded, "I love my grandparents."

"Me too. I mean...they are everyone's grandparents."

He laughed. "Yup. For sure."

I wiped my hands with tissue paper and sipped water. The food was delicious, as expected. Especially the Tarri.

Once we were done, Vihaan pulled out his wallet to pay the bill, but I didn't let him.

"Put that thing back. It's on me."

"Avni..."

"No. You said you'd design my website and I'll show you around. That includes everything. So keep your wallet away." I pointed at his pocket, "Now!"

"Okay fine," he surrendered, reluctantly pocketing his wallet.

I fished out my wallet from the bottom of my bag and paid with cash, tipping the waiter for the service and amazing food. We walked out of the restaurant and were greeted by a whirl of cold breeze. It felt soothing on my skin, finding its way into my hair, pushing the strands away from my face.

"Are you cold?" Vihaan asked, stepping next to me.

"No. I like it. Should we sit for a while?" I pointed at the bench nearby.

"Sure," he walked with me to take a seat.

I didn't want the day to be over. Sitting on the bench was just an excuse to stretch the evening. It would give me more time to spend with him. But the rain had other plans. Just as we were comfortable, the sky above us started rumbling. Lightning struck and dark clouds covered the city.

"We should get going," Vihaan said, getting up from the seat. "Come on." He held out his hand for me to take. It took me a moment to realize that he was asking for me to hold his hand. I swallowed and put my hand on his. He pulled me up to stand and led the way to the nearest bus stop.

"Should we just take a rickshaw?" Vihaan asked as we saw the crowd at the bus stop. "It might rain."

I nodded. At that moment, I just wanted to follow him wherever he wanted to go. He waved at the rickshaw and the driver brought it closer to us. We hopped in, settled down, and informed our destination. The driver put on the meter and started driving. Soon enough, the rain started pouring heavily. The wind was so wild, it was bringing the raindrops inside the rickshaw from both open ends. Vihaan and I had to shift to the center. It brought us so close that our arms brushed together.

Being so close to him made my stomach flip. I was getting nervous. If I look towards him, our faces would be close enough to kiss. But I brushed that thought away and focused on the road ahead. The rickshaw sped on the road, passing by other vehicles.

We reached Rhythm Lane at around 8 in the evening and ran to take shelter at my cafe.

My heart skipped a beat when I found the front door slightly ajar. I could see lights in Reader's Corner. I had checked the door twice before leaving. There was no way I might have left it open. Horrified, I looked at Vihaan. He was as confused as I was.

"Don't worry," he said. "I'll go in first."

Slowly, he opened the door and entered the café. I braced myself as I followed him. But as soon as I was inside, a tiny intruder ran towards me.

"Avu Attu!"

Nidhi wrapped her arms around my waist and gave me a bone-crushing hug. Her whole face was smiling at me as I looked down at her. Vahini and Aai stepped outside, smiling.

"Aai. Vahini? When did you arrive?"

"An hour ago. We wanted to give you a surprise."

"Surprise? You scared me."

I crouched down on my knees and pulled my niece into a gigantic hug. God, I missed her and her apple fragrance shampoo.

"I missed you, Attu," she said, returning my hug even tighter.

"I missed you more, Nidhi."

She giggled and kissed me on both cheeks. I did the same. Aai flicked on the lights and the book cafe illuminated with happiness. Aai smiled at me and then her eyes traveled from me to Vihaan.

"Vihaan? How are you, son?" she asked, smiling at him.

"I'm good, Kaki," he stumbled at each word.

"Have you been helping Avni?" she asked.

"I've been giving her company," he answered. I could sense a slight nervousness in his tone and it was quite adorable.

"So very generous of you. I hope she didn't trouble you much," Aai said rather teasingly.

"Not at all. In fact, she showed me around the city this evening. We are returning from FC road."

"Really?" Vahini added with a cheeky grin. "That's interesting."

"Indeed," Aai said, matching Vahini's tone of teasing. My entire body flushed. It's different when your friends tease you, it's another level when your own mother and sister-in-law tease you.

"How was your journey back home?" I tried to change the topic as I scooped Nidhi in my arms.

"Good good," Aai answered, and turned back to Vihaan. "So Vihaan, how's your new job?"

"Going well, Kaki."

She smiled and asked, "Why don't you join us for dinner?"

"Actually," I interrupted. "We already ate. And don't you want to go home?"

"What's the hurry?" Tanvi Vahini chimed in. "I'm sure you can eat again, won't you?"

Damn you, Vahini.

I looked at Vihaan in an attempt to give him a hint to rescue me from the situation. Aai and Vahini were just teasing. But if they find out my little crush on Vihaan, they'll ask him to marry me on my behalf. That's so not what I want.

"Thank you, Kaki. But I should go. Ajji must be waiting for me." Vihaan managed a steady voice as he humbly replied.

"We can call them too," Vahini suggested.

"No!" I firmly added. "We should go home. Nidhi must be tired and I have a surprise for her." I remembered the sling bag I got for her at the right moment.

"Really? What is it?"

"I'll show you once we get home."

"Let's go home, Aai," she pleaded. "Ajji, hurry."

My little trick worked. Nidhi was so excited that she dragged us all out of the cafe.

"Bye Vihaan Dada," she waved at him. "We will see you tomorrow."

He chuckled and pulled her cheeks, "Bye Nidhi. Can't wait to see you again."

When Nupur brought my pets back, we all walked home. I was glad that Nidhi was talking too much and I didn't have to face my mother's questions. Nidhi told me everything that happened in a couple of days in her life in a single breath. I listened as she mimicked the people she met. Once home, she didn't let me go to my room. She wanted me to help her into pajamas and then show her surprise. So I obeyed as any cool aunt would do.

Her eyes went as wide as her smile when she saw the sling bag. She jumped in joy and ran all around the house carrying her new bag.

"This is for you, Vahini and Aai." I handed them the new wallets I had gotten for them.

"Oh, I love it," Vahini beamed. "Thank you, Avu."

"My purse is perfectly fine. Why did you have to get a new one?" Aai critically glanced at the wallet.

Vahini giggled. I shook my head. "Your purse is probably 5 years old. Use this one from now on." Aai argued for a while but eventually agreed to use her new wallet.

Nidhi was still chirping around us, singing songs and telling stories that she learned from her grandparents. Vahini let her jump around.

"She'll get tired and sleep," Vahini whispered to me with a chuckle. Finally, after half an hour, Nidhi yawned and declared that we should all go to bed now.

"Good night, Nidhi." I kissed her cheeks and went into my room. Changing into pajamas, I slid under my warm blanket, happy to lay down. It was a tiring day, but the most amazing day of my life. I felt relaxed after a long time.

My phone chimed with a new message from Vihaan.

Vihaan: Thanks for the evening. It was fun.

Me: My pleasure. I had fun too.

Vihaan: Good night. I'll see you tomorrow.

Me: Good night, Vihaan.

With Vihaan's thoughts circling in my head, I closed my eyes, cherishing the moments of the day. It was our first date, at least I believed so. For me, a date is not about a candlelight dinner at a fancy restaurant where you can't even pronounce half of the menu. It's about spending time with the right person in a chaotic bus, clicking selfies, and laughing until your tummy hurts.

SIXTEEN

Has anyone ever complimented you for being weird? I bet not. But I have been receiving such compliments quite often from Vihaan. I mean, I consider it as a compliment. Since I coerced him into buddy reading a Romance novel with me, he has gotten grumpy. We've read only the first four chapters so far. But it's too soon for him to get along with the book. He keeps promising he will finish it, but I doubt that.

As my family returned home last night, Vihaan didn't spend his entire day in my café. He just stopped by in the morning to say Hi. I missed him the whole day and almost thought he was sitting by the counter as I cooked. How quickly I got used to having him around me. For the whole day, I thought something was not right. It was his presence that I craved.

Aai and Vahini wanted to invite him for our evening tea, but I distracted them by showing new book arrangements until they decided to go home claiming they were tired. After they left, I brewed lemongrass tea and brought the tray of teapot and cups out, waiting for Rutu and Nupur to arrive.

"We need chai," the girls announced even before entering the café.

"On it," I yelled back and poured tea into cups.

Both of them dropped themselves on the sofa and huffed a relief.

"Love the new look," Rutu appreciatively glanced around.

"I know right? Check out my new teapots."

"Tulshibaug?" Nupur asked.

"Yup," I replied with a grin.

This morning, I hung some more fairy lights that I bought from Tulashibaug. Twinkly decorative items were outlining the windows. Books on the shelves were accompanied by new teapots and showpieces.

Slowly, my book cafe is turning into a better and more graceful version of itself. I'm seeing my dream spread out in front of me. This is exactly how I wanted it to look. But whenever I feel certain about my plans for the café, the date of returning Madhav kaka's money stares back at me. I did save some money through catering and nooks. Apart from Shweta's group, a lady from a neighboring society has booked a nook for the next month and I have at least 3 more bookings coming up. I'm hoping for the best.

Nupur took a sip and shifted in her seat to face me, "How was your date?"

I sighed as my nosy friends looked at me with wicked smiles. I knew they must be dying to ask me about last evening.

"It was good," I replied.

"Just good?" Rutu raised an eyebrow. "From what we see on your face, it was pretty great."

Why my face has to reflect all my feelings for everyone to notice? I tried my best to not smile but failed. How could I hide it from them? They are my best friends after all.

"It was amazing," I told them. "We had so much fun."

"And did you tell him?" Nupur asked excitedly.

"What?"

"That you like him?"

"God no," I whispered as if Vihaan could somehow hear me.

"Why not?" Rutu leaned back and sipped her chai. "We were hoping you did and we'll be free to tease you both."

"I didn't. I don't know how to tell him."

Both of them went silent for a moment as they considered my thoughts. I honestly have no idea how to tell him, or do I even want to tell him? Sharing such raw feelings and being vulnerable with someone sounds terrifying. How would he react? If we're not on the same page, it'll break my heart for sure. And I'm absolutely not ready for that.

"You have to tell him, eventually," Nupur softly said. "I mean...you clearly like him. Why not..."

"What if he doesn't feel the same?" I interrupted her. "It will ruin everything we have right now."

"That's everyone's fear, Avni. But if you really like him, you have to tell him. And what if he feels the same? Think about it," Rutu said like an elder sister, resting her hand on mine. "We are happy for you that you found someone. You can't let that go, okay? You don't find love that often. When you do, you at least have to let them know."

I nodded, considering the possibility of him liking me back. How much that will make me happy.

"Anyways," I said, "We should plan a girl's day out soon. It's been a long time."

"Yes!" Nupur almost jumped out of her seat. "I'm bored. We should do something fun."

"What are you guys planning?" Prachiti's voice emerged from the door. She entered the café followed by Vihaan and whom I assumed must be Nishant, Prachiti's brother.

Vihaan was carrying his laptop under his arm. He gave me a soft smile before greeting my friends. Rutu and Nupur looked at me, hoping to see me blush or do something stupid. But I was surprisingly calm.

"Hi Prachiti," I greeted her. "And you must be Nishant. Nice to meet you."

"Likewise." He smiled and shook my hand. "I've heard a lot about you." He cocked his head to glance at Vihaan and quickly added, "My sister tells me so much about you and your book café."

"Glad to know that. We are having chai, would you guys like some?" I offered. When three of them nodded, I brought more cups out.

"How come you are here man?" Vihaan asked, taking the cup from me and handing one to Nishant.

"Oh. My sister has some news to share," he shook his head. "Apparently it couldn't wait and she didn't want to convey it over the phone. So here I am."

Prachiti beamed at me. Her eyes shone through her spectacles.

"Okay. What is it?" Nupur asked impatiently.

Prachiti sat on the chair and began talking so fast, I struggled to keep up. "So the thing is, my college is hosting a tech event, Technofest, this Sunday. All engineering colleges in Pune are going to participate. Lots of students, professors, and some startup founders will be there. And my college is inviting local businesses to set up a stall at the event. Anything that students can buy. And local journalists are going to cover every aspect of it, including the stalls."

She paused to catch her breath and continued. "It'll be awesome if you all could come."

"We would love to," Rutu replied, her voice filled with excitement. "What's the procedure to participate?"

Prachiti bit her tongue, "Actually. I knew you'd say yes. So I already booked three stalls for you. Seats are limited, so I figured..."

"Fantastic," Nupur leaned in her seat and pulled Prachiti in a hug.

"I will share the pamphlet with you soon," Prachiti grinned, happy with our positive response.

"Thank you Prachiti," I pulled her cheek. "I'm sure we'll have fun."

"And," she concluded. "I am going to be your coordinator. So I'll be helping you during the event."

"That's even better," I cheered.

Over the past couple of weeks, Prachiti became our good friend. She stopped by quite a few times to buy books and now she's one of us.

"We have a lot to prepare," Nupur chimed in. "We have to create a list of things we need."

"Yes and we have to decide what we're going to wear," Rutu added. "You two must let me choose your outfits."

"I'll have to go grocery shopping," I prompted.

"This conversation will never end." Vihaan shook his head.

Nishant only chuckled.

And I was just happy to be with my favorite people. The evening quickly turned vibrant as we chatted about the event that sounded like a big deal. Maybe, this event can change everything for my café.

"Prachiti. Look it's going to rain. We should go home," Nishant said to his little sister, patiently. Seeing them together flooded my heart with memories of me and Harsh Dada. He too was patient with me, always. Even if I sometimes fought, Dada teased me but never fought with me.

"Don't be silly. Better stay indoors until the sky clears out. How about I make *Kanda Bhaji*?" I offered.

Suddenly, everybody cheered as if I offered to host a feast. Kanda Bhaji with my friends as it rained and brought the fragrance of moist soil sounded like a perfect plan.

"I'll help," Rutu stood up.

"Me too," Nupur added.

"No," I pushed them back down on the sofa. "You guys talk. Maybe start creating a list of things that we'll need for the event. I'll be back before you know it."

Nupur's eyes lit up. She hurried to the counter to grab a pen and paper. She, Prachiti, and Rutu started scribbling notes as I went into the kitchen.

I wore my apron and began slicing onions. Marinating the onions with salt to induce moisture, I kept them aside and started chopping green chilies and coriander. Once the onions were moist enough, I added gram flour, some rice flour, green chili, coriander, cumin seeds, a pinch of turmeric, and sprinkled a little bit of water to create a semi-dry dough. The oil was perfectly hot by the time I started frying Bhajis.

"Smells amazing!" Nupur yelled from outside. I smiled and served crispy Kanda Bhaji on the plate with chutney and fried green chili sprinkled with salt.

When I placed the tray on the table, everybody picked up their plate with delight.

"Avni, I love you," Rutu declared, stuffing her mouth with bhaji. I turned to look at Vihaan to see his reaction. He took a bite and raised an appreciative eyebrow at me.

"It's perfect," he whispered. Everyone showered compliments as they ate with delight. Outside, the rain drizzled with rhythmic noise. Chaturvedi Ajoba waved at me from his dairy. A cheery smile on his face.

"I'll be back." I went into the kitchen and packed a parcel of Kanda Bhaji for Chaturvedi Ajji and Ajoba. Grabbing my umbrella from behind the counter, I walked across the street to his dairy.

"Ajoba, fresh Kanda Bhaji. Hope you'll like it."

His smile widened as he opened the box. "Smells amazing." He dipped the bhaji into chutney and took a bite. "Delicious. Now go get inside."

I chuckled and walked back to join my friends. Vihaan looked at me. His face broke into a gentle smile. I realized, there were some raindrops on my cheeks. I wiped them away and grabbed my plate of Bhaji.

We all sat together, eating Kanda bhaji and making silly jokes. Teasing each other and making plans for Sunday's event. Even though I have so many things to figure out, so much going on in my life, the future of my book cafe is still uncertain, but sitting among my friends, I forgot everything. I was present at the moment, imprinting every little detail in my mind so I'll recall it in the future. The entire Rhythm Lane has enveloped me in so much love, I wouldn't need anything else.

When I looked at Vihaan, he was enjoying himself. He seemed relaxed and happy. Now he has somewhere to call his home, with his friends and family by his side. He doesn't have to change cities just when he starts to like it there. He can stay here as long as he wants.

"Alright. Now we should get going." Nishant wiped his hands with tissue paper. "Aai must be waiting for us."

"Yes. Of course." Prachiti got up from her seat and gave me a hug, "Bhaji was wonderful, Avni Di. Thank you."

"Yeah. Truly." Nishant smiled at me. "How much do we owe you?"

"It's on me. I'm just happy you all had fun."

"No no, please," he insisted and ended up paying for everyone. "We'll see you all again soon."

Everybody bid goodbye to each other. We all decided that we will plan another such evening soon. When Nishant and Prachiti left, Nupur and Rutu got up to leave too.

Rutu leaned closer to me and whispered in my ears, "Tell him," and hurried across the lane with Nupur to resume their work. I turned to see Vihaan, hoping he hadn't heard what Rutu said. I was thankful when I saw him powering on his laptop.

When he saw me glancing at him, he smiled and said, "I have something to show you. Come join me."

SEVENTEEN

"Oh my god. When did you do it?"

When Vihaan said he wanted to show me something, I knew it would be about my website but I didn't expect it to be nearly ready. I thought he would need at least a week to design it. When I joined him on the sofa and watched as he typed *amongthepages.com* on the search bar, I braced myself. The website was nothing like what I had imagined. It was much much better.

"Last night," he informed. "It's no big deal. I used a template and customized it a little to your liking."

"This is amazing," I beamed at him. It truly was amazing. The homepage had animations of dogs and books. A few pictures of the café's interior were auto-scrolling on the header. There were four tabs in the side menu- Home, About Us, Books & Food, and Subscribe to Bookbox. He showed me each page one by one. The *Books & Food* page had sample products to add to the cart. "We can add everything in the database later," he told me as he scrolled through the page. The About Us page was empty except for a few pictures and social media handles. Out of all the pages, I loved the book-box subscription page. It was vibrant and simple. He had created three dummy subscriptions and a *Subscribe To Happiness* button below it. "We have to mention details for each subscription. How many books and what kind of food items a box will have, that sort of things," he said, scrolling to the bottom of the page.

The footer section was equally amazing. Vihaan had created the 'Join the Book Club' field which will notify me if anyone wants to join a book club. "You mentioned you wanted to start a book club that Prachiti can host? We can integrate those details here."

Everything on the website was more than amazing. I didn't know he could do it so quickly and so well.

"I don't know what to say," I confessed. "I love it."

He smiled at me. "I'm glad. And we can do more, this is just the base of it."

"Thank you so much."

"Don't mention it. I'm glad I could help."

I asked him if I could open the website on my phone and he said I absolutely could. So when I typed the site address on the search bar, it opened in the mobile version.

"This is so cool," I rejoiced. An idea came to my mind as I scrolled through the website. "How about we call it *Our Story* instead of *About us?* And, maybe we can add a feature to create custom book boxes for people? Choose any 10 books and we can decide the price accordingly?"

"We can do that," Vihaan confirmed. "First we will have to add all books into the database. That we can do over the week. You can do it too, I'll show you how to."

"Okay," I smiled, still scrolling through my new website.

As we were discussing my website, a loud noise somewhere nearby made me flinch. The power outage wrapped darkness around the entire lane. Soon, the wind started whirling as the light drizzle turned into heavy rain.

"Great!" I groaned, annoyed at the sudden change of events. "What do we do now?"

"Relax," Vihaan turned on the torch of his phone. "Do you happen to have candles here?"

"Oh. As it happens," I answered, "I have scented ones."

Vihaan followed me with his phone's torch as I fiddled inside all the drawers under the counter until I found my favorite lavender-scented candle jar and lit it up with a matchbox. The fragrance of lavender enveloped us as I kept it on the tea table. When Vihaan turned off his phone's torch, everything went dim for a moment until our eyes adjusted to the gentle glow from the candle.

In a dimly lit room, he looked so good. So handsome and calm. I was tempted to touch his face, run my fingers through his hair, hold his hand and interlock our fingers, relive the moment when I ran into his arms and he held me close.

Instead, I sat on the other end of the sofa, keeping a safe distance from him. He leaned back and told me that he is going to integrate the payment gateway on my website soon.

My phone vibrated on my lap with Aai's message. *Avu, are you okay?*

I quickly replied to her that I'm safe and Vihaan is accompanying me. Once she was satisfied with my response, I focused back on Vihaan.

"What else do you want to do on the website?" he asked, opening the backend code of the website.

I gave it a thought. There's one thing that I always wanted to do, Baba's books.

"I want to create a separate section for my Baba's books. We do sell his books here whenever we can. But if I can create his author profile on this website, his stories will still remain in this world."

Vihaan's expressions were calm and understanding when he listened to me. He shifted slightly closer to me, comforting me with his presence.

I continued, remembering my Dada, "I also want to upload a few old pictures on *Our Story* page. Dada and I created so many fun memories here."

He nodded, giving me a gentle smile, "Sure. We can do that."

I looked to my right to glance at our old family picture on the shelf. It's a candid picture of all of us laughing. I still remember how Baba and Dada used to sound when they laughed. How Dada's face would turn red if he laughed too much. How happy we all were.

A tiny tear escaped my eyes and I quickly dabbed a tissue paper to trap the tears flooding my cheeks. Vihaan looked at me with concern. He didn't know what to say to me, how to handle such a delicate situation.

I wiped my eyes in an attempt to collect myself. Vihaan's gaze was steady on mine. He hesitated before saying, "I'm here...if you wanna talk about it." His tone was gentle and careful.

I looked down at my lap, trying to map words that I wanted to say out loud. Things that I haven't shared with anyone in a while. Aai, Vahini, and I talked very little about it. Only occasionally. We mostly busy ourselves so we won't overthink. My heart started bubbling up with all the unsaid feelings.

I cleared my throat and mumbled, "I still can't believe they are not here. I don't think any of us has fully come to terms with it."

He nodded but didn't say anything, giving me time to let out my thoughts.

"This place used to bloom back in days when...you know. Always busy."

My voice got caught in my throat. But tonight, I wanted to talk about it. Or I would never be strong enough to embrace the truth, however painful it is.

"My Baba wanted both readers and writers to have a place to call their own. Somewhere to escape when they much needed it. That's what we did in our bookstore. Readers and writers were free to share their thoughts, and plan events to build communities. It was all glorious...until one day, Baba and Dada never returned home."

Vihaan shifted in his seat. He was close to me yet far enough to let me have my space.

"What saddens me most is, they didn't get to see all this. They would never know what happened to their bookstore. Dada would never be able to see Nidhi growing up and I..." I paused to draw a deep breath, "I don't know if I'm doing good. I want to keep this store running as long as I can. I don't want to..." I paused again. I knew if I shared too much, I might blurt out about Madhav Kaka. Nobody needs to know about it yet. It's a family matter and I don't even want to burden my family with it, let alone Vihaan.

"Anyway," I eventually said as I gathered myself. "I'll ask Baba's publisher to reprint his books so we can put them on the website."

Vihaan gave me a gentle smile. His eyes were calm and soothing. I wanted to lose in them never to find my way back out again. I felt safe with him, knowing he would be here. I wanted to talk more, but I didn't have the courage to continue the conversation. Words are not enough to tell how much I miss my father and brother.

Silence hovered between us for a moment. None of us knew what to say next. I understood his reluctance though, so I decided to change the direction of our conversation to lighten up the mood.

"How's your app going?"

My question took him off guard, but he smiled, "I think it's going good. I made progress."

"Can I see it?"

"Soon," he replied.

"Okay," I nodded. "I'm proud of you. Both for app and my website."

He chuckled, "I'm flattered. And I'm happy I resumed working on my app."

"I'm glad you did. You'll be a famous coder one day, like Mark Zuckerberg," I beamed at him.

He laughed from his heart and I joined in, feeling light as I laughed with him. He looked me in the eyes. His gaze lingered between my eyes and my lips. He fell silent and gulped. I could see his adam's apple bobbing in his throat.

"What happened?" I asked as his face turned serious.

"Avni I..."

"What? Are you feeling alright?" Panic rushed through me as he suddenly became so serious.

He rested his hand on my arm, slowly, and said, "I've been meaning to tell you something. This is probably not the right time. But I just have to."

I frowned impatiently, "Yeah go ahead."

His gaze on mine wasn't the one I usually noticed. It was different and deep. He wasn't even blinking. I didn't know what to do or say, so I looked down at his hand on mine.

"No," he lifted my chin. "Don't look away. Look at me."

Now I was worried. My heart started beating faster.

"Okay," I whispered. "I won't look away."

He kept his eyes on mine. His hand brushed from my arm to my palm and he interlinked our fingers together, exactly what I wanted to do some time ago. I braced myself, for what he had to say was going to melt my heart. I could feel it.

He took a deep breath before telling me the one thing that will make my heart race every time I'll recall this evening in my mind.

"The day I arrived here," he began. "I was looking forward to seeing you. I thought about you a lot, wondered how you looked now. But then you didn't recognize me, and to be honest, I was disappointed. Later on, you were so welcoming, even in your weird rivalry ways, forcing me to read one of your romance books," he chuckled, "that I fell for you, Avni. So much that it's all about you now. And, seeing you work so hard for your dreams, for your family, made me realize, how much I needed to work on my own dreams." He took a moment to collect his thoughts, tightening his grip around my fingers. "I don't want to wait anymore to tell you how much I love you. More than I could put in words, more than anything. You changed my life. You made me realize that this is my home. This lane, where my family lives, where *you* live. And I am going to stay here even if you get annoyed at me and ask me to leave."

My jaw dropped slightly. I blinked and swallowed. I was running low on words. Is that how he's been feeling all along? Am I the one who didn't understand his hints? I thought, him spending time here, or helping me, is all out of friendship. I've never been so wrong in my life.

"I..." I began talking, but couldn't. Corners of my eyes filled with tears without me realizing it.

"Hey," Vihaan shifted closer to me. "Don't cry. I didn't mean to upset you. I'm sorry, Avni. I know this must be a lot to take. You can ignore everything I just said if you want to."

"No," I managed to whisper. "I don't want to."

"What?"

"I don't want to ignore it."

"Oh," he mumbled, waiting for me to catch up.

"Didn't you see?" I asked. "Never on my face or eyes?"

"What?" he scanned my face to find answers.

"Didn't you see how much I was in love with you all this time? Nupur and Rutu said that my face said it all."

He fell silent for a moment, processing my confession.

"I dropped so many hints. I thought you were just trying to be a good friend."

"No," he shook his head. "I thought...Well, I didn't want to put you in an awkward situation."

"Why would I force you to read a romance book with me?"

He chuckled, looking down at our interlocked hands, "That makes sense."

"Still you didn't get my hint."

"Okay, I'm sorry." The corners of his lips lifted, putting a perfect smile on his handsome face.

"Anyway," I continued. "My point is. I love you too. I've been trying to...well glad to know you love me too," I sniffled and wiped my eyes. "Do you mean it though?"

He lifted my hand and brought it closer to his lips. Planting a soft kiss on my knuckles, he replied, "Every word I said."

"Good," I wiped away the last of my tears.

He got up from the seat and stood in front of me. The candlelight flickered over the wind slipping through the window, casting a glow on Vihaan's face. I could see his smile and his sparkly brown eyes. I could see him extending his arms to both sides and nodding at me, asking me to fall into them. It took me a moment to get up, but when I did, I threw myself at him, wrapping my arms around his neck, losing myself into him, melting into his arms, falling apart and collecting back. He chuckled when I hugged him tightly. "Easy. I'm not going anywhere."

"You better not." I tucked my face under his jaw.

He lifted me up from the floor, his hands tight around my waist, and whispered in my ears, "You are so crazy, Avni Joshi."

"Yes fine, I love you too, Vihaan Chaturvedi," I whispered back.

He laughed and gave me a tight hug before gently putting me back on the ground.

"Your eyes are beautiful," Vihaan held my gaze. I lowered my eyelashes and smiled.

I was both excited and scared for the moment that I saw coming. He tugged my chin upwards, lowered his face, and brushed his lips lightly on mine before pulling them into a kiss. Closing my eyes, I lost myself in the moment as he kissed me. Gentle and sweet. I raised my toes to match his height. He held me closer.

Just when I was melting into him, my phone chimed again, shattering a beautiful moment. He chuckled and planted a gentle kiss on my forehead. I frowned as he freed himself away from me. But I had to check my phone. "It must be Aai again," I whispered and unlocked my phone.

When I saw the notification, whatever little glow I had on my face vanished. My heart started racing for completely wrong reasons. I sat down, dreading to read the full message.

Madhav Kaka: I will be visiting soon. Please keep half of the amount ready.

I kept my phone aside and tried to calm down but couldn't. The partial amount was still big. We could arrange it, but not without facing unnecessary stress. Tears blurred my vision as I tried to think a way through it.

Vihaan sat next to me, worried and confused. "What happened Avni? Is everything okay?"

"Nothing is okay," I muttered between my sobs. Vihaan pulled me closer, wrapping his arms around me. I hugged him and without wasting any moment, told him everything, right from the beginning. His expressions shifted from concern to rage back to concern as he listened to me.

"What? Why didn't you tell me?"

"Nobody knows about it except my family."

Vihaan rubbed his temple, "This is outrageous. You should...anyway...we can figure it out okay? Don't worry."

I nodded, wiping my eyes. Did he send a similar message to Aai or Vahini? If yes, both of them will panic and try to arrange money by breaking their savings. And if not, I won't tell them until I find a permanent solution to put an end to all of it.

I looked at Vihaan. He was as concerned as I was. I needed to do something quickly. Anything.

"Can you drop me home?" I asked.

"Of course. Anything you want," he replied.

EIGHTEEN

When Vihaan dropped me home, Aai was waiting for me in the living room. Claiming a headache, I told her I'll go upstairs and get some sleep. She didn't let me go without shoving a glass of warm turmeric milk in my hand. "Drink it Avu, you'll feel better." I took the glass from her with a smile in an attempt to hide my fear. Giving her a hug and saying goodnight, I made my way upstairs.

Madhav Kaka's sudden message shook me. I was going to request an extension on his deadline as I still don't have enough money. Now I don't know what am I supposed to do. The deadline is still a month away and now he wants half of the amount soon.

Panicked, I paced through my room thinking there must be something that I can do. Prachiti's college event is in two days, I would earn some money there. But again, everything together isn't nearly closer to half of his asked amount.

Tons of thoughts flooded my mind. This is the second time Madhav Kaka ruined a perfectly beautiful day for me. Why does he need to set a deadline? It's not like we're running away with his money. I can pay him back in installments if only he could wait for a while.

The more I thought about it, the more I wondered- why is he so desperate to get money? I've been thinking about it since the day he decided to show up claiming his rights.

Why now?

And the answer was right there. He desperately needs money for some urgent reasons. That's the only possible explanation I could think of. He needs money and he thought this would be the easiest way to get it.

I stopped pacing and sat down on my bed with a turmeric milk glass still in my hand. Aai made it with love, to make sure I'll feel okay. I sniffed the milk's aroma and gulped a long sip, thinking about what to do next. If I plan something, millions of things could go wrong. But I can't just sit back and panic.

Baba. What would my Baba do? He always used to maintain his calm. I don't remember ever seeing him panic. He used to say to Dada and me quite often, "You should control your thoughts, not the other way around. You must write your thoughts every day to get them out."

I took out his diary from my bag and sat back down to leaf through his thoughts. His soothing words might help me come up with a solution. I was dreading the moment it will bring me to the last entry and I'll be heartbroken. But I was determined to read, hoping Baba would guide me somehow.

I resumed reading from where I left it last time and read every single word imagining Baba's voice. By the time I reached 29th March 2018, Baba's diary entry made me sit straight in my bed. Between those pages, I found something none of us knew about.

~

March 29, 2018

Madhav Bhau stopped by last evening, this time with a new proposal. He told me that one of his friends is willing to invest in our bookstore and that he wants to join us. I said I'm not looking for more investors and I want the store to remain within the family.

Madhav Bhau wouldn't let go of the topic, so I told him I'll think about it. At least that stopped him from trying to persuade me.

His coming up with new proposals every now and then is making me question his intentions. Tomorrow he'll say something new and won't let it go until I put a complete stop to it.

Now I think, it would be better if I return his money with interest and free up 25% that belongs to him. I should have done it years ago when I started to get hints that Madhav Bhau isn't actually interested in the bookstore.

Better now than never. I do have enough savings and my new book's royalty to return his investment. Some of the savings were for Avni's café, but for now, it's important to secure the bookstore's future and make it debt-free. I can write more books, and earn more money.

Once I return his money and complete the legal procedure, he won't bother my family again.

~

I knew it. Baba wouldn't keep problems for too long. He would get rid of it before his family could even know about it. I should have read his diary long ago and this wouldn't have happened. I would have confronted Madhav Kaka. But now that he is using illegal documents against us, I need solid proof too. Baba's diary entry won't work. There's only one place where I'll find the proof. The bank transactions. If Baba completed the procedure, there should be a transaction entry about it.

I quickly powered on my laptop and logged into the bookstore's bank account. Inputting 2018 in the filter, I hit submit to see all the transactions. I scanned the amount column, skipping the small transactions and only focusing on bigger ones. To my disappointment, all the entries were either about book consignments or bulk book purchases. None of the transactions was credited to Madhav Kaka's account. If Baba didn't use the store's account, how did he send money?

Then it hit me. He must have used his personal savings account. He didn't want anyone of us to know about it until he had all the necessary documents.

Baba's savings account will definitely have some proof of transaction. My Baba wasn't much tech-savvy. Our bookstore account has internet banking because Dada set it up. Baba's book royalty account and his personal account didn't have internet banking. He regularly updated his passbooks from the bank. His passbooks will have the transaction entry between him and Kaka.

If I want to get Baba's passbook, I have to go to Aai's room. She sleeps light and I'm sure she'll wake up if I go there right now. I have to wait until morning and do it without her knowledge.

Sighing, I kept everything aside and slid under my blanket. It was the longest night of my life. I didn't fall asleep at all. I felt confident that I will find a permanent solution. That anxiety of rush kept me awake.

When Aai and Vahini were leaving to drop Nidhi off at school in the morning, I told them to open the cafe without me.

"I'll join a little later today, Aai. I'm not feeling well."

She offered to stay home with me, but I brushed her worries away.

"Call me if you need anything," Vahini told me before leaving. I kissed Nidhi on the cheek and waved at them from the doorway before hurrying into Aai's room.

Baba's bank document binder was exactly where he used to keep it, in the bottom drawer of his study table. I sat on Aai's bed and opened the binder to find a bunch of Bank Passbooks tied with a rubber band. I opened each to find the one from 2018. There was only one passbook for that year with entries till April, the month Baba must have printed it for the last time.

I leafed through the passbook until entries from March began and scanned each transaction till the end of April. There were only a few entries to check, so it didn't take me much time to arrive at the one I was looking for. Baba had, indeed, returned Madhav Kaka's money on the 16th of April. I grabbed a pen from the desk and circled the transaction entry that will change everything. My heart started racing. Adrenaline rushed through my veins. I found the proof. I did it.

But what about the final documents? Baba's entire folder or his drawers didn't have any document that said he removed Madhav Kaka from the store's ownership. There has to be a legal document somewhere. If I found this, I'm sure I can find that too. But first, I needed to go to the café.

Nupur has been texting me all morning to join her and Rutu to plan Technofest. We needed to organize a bunch of things to carry to the event on Sunday. Vahini told me she would handpick books for me to take. My stall is going to have both books and food to sell and I needed to prepare the special menu card.

And as far as the documents are concerned, I have an idea that might work. Aai and Vahini don't need to know anything about it yet. Not until I can tell them, confidently, that our bookstore is going to be ours without paying anyone anything. I hope it all works out.

By the time I reached the café, Vahini was already sorting books for me. My pets circled her as she showed them books and they woofed an approval.

"How do you feel?" she asked when she saw me enter. Aai turned her attention from her book to me.

"Good, I guess. I'll feel better after a cup of tea. Want some?"

Both of them nodded with a soft smile on their faces. Smile that I wish would never get wiped.

I brewed extra chai, knowing my friends would barge in anytime now. As expected, Nupur and Rutu made an overly dramatic and loud arrival, asking why I was late for the most important meeting of our lives.

"I wanted to prepare myself for your loud screeching," I told Nupur. "Now here we are."

Rutu laughed and sat on the rug next to Vahini. Nupur and I squeezed ourselves into the free space and we all started planning the event.

Sipping tea with my friends and family, I scribbled notes. My grocery list wasn't that big, but I needed help. Vihaan offered to get groceries sorted for both me and Nupur, who needed an enormous amount of eggs and flour to bake cakes in advance.

After last night's confession and kiss, Vihaan and I didn't get a chance to talk. But he understood it. He didn't ask a single question about Madhav Kaka in front of my family. He smiled at me and said, "Don't worry. I'm right here with you."

I had to fight back tears when he said that. I wanted to hug him but not when four pairs of eyes were watching us. Instead, I smiled at him and handed over the grocery list.

Our To-Do list extended four pages, making it harder to track. Vahini declared she will get the pamphlets sorted for all of us. She settled with my laptop and designed simple pamphlets on the same graphic design app that I use.

Our day went by faster than light. At some point in the evening, Prachiti stopped by to wish us luck and gave us the booklet that had all the information about our stall numbers, our entry passes, and the timetable of the event.

Rutu spent the entire evening ironing clothes, stitching last-minute adjustments, and packing bags of clothes, scarves, scrunchies, and handmade bags.

We still weren't fully packed when we all sat for dinner on the rug in the middle of the café. Nupur's parents, Vihaan and Chaturvedi Ajji-Ajoba joined us for dinner and lent us helping hands to pack our stuff.

I was the only one who needed a gas stove, which didn't seem comfortable. Thankfully, Doctor Kaka had an Induction that I could use. I anyway was going to prepare most of it in the café, so an Induction would do.

Soon, the evening turned into night. Tired, everyone left home except for me, Nupur, Rutu, and Vahini. Aai took Nidhi and our pets home, promising to return early in the morning.

By the time we were partially done packing, it was 1 AM.

"We still have tomorrow to pack the rest of it," Nupur said, rubbing her tired neck. None of us had any energy left to go home, so instead, we all ladies ended up sleeping in my bookhouse, looking forward to Sunday's event.

NINETEEN

"Avni! Let's go!" Nupur yelled at top of her lungs from her cake shop. Rutu was already waiting outside with her bags, wearing a long maroon maxi skirt paired with a white t-shirt and denim jacket. Her hair was tied in a messy bun, accessorized with a sparkly hair clip. She asked Nupur to wear a light yellow puff sleeve top over jeans. 'It somehow matches your cupcakes,' she suggested with a giggle. And I was told to wear my peach-colored short kurta over jeans. Vahini tied my hair in a french braid and pulled out a couple of strands to outline my cheeks. "You look cute." Nidhi kissed me on both cheeks. I hugged her and dragged my stuff outside the café to be loaded into Chaturvedi Ajoba's minivan. Vihaan was going to drop us all at the event, and then drive to Nishant's home to do some work on his App.

CVR Engineering College is merely a 5-minute long drive. We decided to leave half an hour prior to set up our stalls. As we all squeezed ourselves into the minivan, everybody wished us luck and gave too many instructions. Vihaan started the engine and drove us to the college. When we reached, Prachiti was already waiting by the gate to welcome us.

The College is pretty big. The moment you enter through the main gate, tall buildings for various engineering departments surround you. There's a beautiful garden in the center and a massive sports ground ahead of it where 20 stalls were outlining the circular edge. A quick glance around told me that there were stalls selling stationery, engineering products, hardware, hand-painted vases, backpacks, and even shoes. At least 6 stalls were selling food, including mine. Bhel Puri, Vada Pav, Burgers, Dosa. There was one fruit-juice stall too. A huge canopy was built at the center of the ground where the Technofest event was supposed to be happening in half an hour.

Together, all of us settled each of our stalls and hung the sign of our Store names on the front hook.

"Smile!" Vihaan angled his phone camera in front of us. We girls smiled and posed as he clicked pictures.

As I arranged all my utensils, Vihaan made sure my Induction, Toaster, Kettle, and Blender were working properly. "You look beautiful," he whispered into my ears before leaving. "I'll come back for lunch to attend the rest of the event," he told me.

"Okay," I whispered back. "I'll wait for you." He jogged towards the van and turned around to smile at me before driving away.

This morning, I got up at 5 to prepare all the ingredients. I created a special menu for the event which includes Sandwiches, Rolls, Omelettes, Quick Bites, and of course, chai and coffee. I kept my denim apron on the counter, pulled out a stack of paper plates, glasses, and ketchup sachets from the boxes, and kept them on the side counter to be prepared.

The portable book cart I had brought was decorated with twinkly stars, plants, and stickers of fictional figures. I unboxed my book box and arranged all 50 books that I had brought to sell.

Soon, the announcement was made on stage under the canopy- *Technofest will start in 10 minutes.* Prachiti, who was carrying a notepad and some papers, asked us to sign on the entry sheet and disappeared among other volunteers.

She returned with another sheet with more sets of instructions. "Let's see. An introductory session from 10 to 10:30. People might roam around to get some tea or cold drinks," she looked at me when she said that, indicating I should be prepared. "Some local reporters and journalists are joining us to cover the event and they might ask you some questions about your businesses. Don't hesitate to advertise yourselves," she grinned. "Everyone will eventually visit stalls for lunch or snacks. That's all. You get to see the whole event and do business. Nothing to worry about."

I huffed a loud sigh and looked at my friends. It's going to be a busy day and we were looking forward to it.

"Alright ladies." Rutu adjusted her hair. "Let's do this."

As soon as the event began, I turned on the Coffee kettle as Chai was brewing on the induction. While I arranged sandwiches, both the beverages were done. I poured them into thermoses and kept them on the counter.

I had already prepared the stuffing for the rolls and quick bites in containers. All the ingredients were set for the day so whenever an order comes, I could serve hot meals.

In a stall to my right, Nupur creatively displayed her cupcakes and pastries on cake stands. Her counter was colorful and delicious. When I turned to look at Rutu, she was pairing sling bags and scarves with tops to be displayed. Her fashion accessories were arranged on the counter in cute boxes.

Giving each other encouraging smiles, we all waited to see what was going to happen during the event. Engineering students from all over Pune gathered around with their professors. One by one, a group of students were presenting their projects in front of an audience. Out of all the groups, five were going to win a sponsorship or an opportunity to work in a startup. From amazing apps to smart robots, we saw a lot of new things. I couldn't believe these students could build so many amazing things. Vihaan would have loved it. I missed him as I watched students present the features of their apps.

After the first 10 presentations, students started roaming around to shop. A group of girls approached Rutu to buy scarves and trendy tops. She helped them pair various accessories and gave fashion tips. Another group of girls and boys, with their 3 professors approached my stall. I greeted them with a cheery smile.

"Hello. What would you like to have?"

One of the female professors stepped forward. "Three cups of tea please, and students want some cold coffee. And," she scanned the menu card hooked to the frame of the stall and turned to her students, "what would you like to have?"

Excited, students ordered a bunch of things. Bombay masala Sandwiches, Paneer Rolls, and Cheese potato pockets.

"Give me 5 minutes." I smiled at them. "Feel free to browse books." I placed a pan on my induction as I toasted sandwiches in the toaster. When the pan was warm enough, I drizzled some oil on it and placed wheat chapatti paneer rolls to catch the crisp. Side by side, I was able to fry potato pockets and serve everything with beverages on the side. The group started eating with delight, sharing food with each other.

"Chai is fantastic," the female professor said to me as she took a sip. "What's in it with ginger?"

"Lemongrass," I told her with a smile. "Glad you like it."

I glanced at Nupur. She was serving pastries and packing cupcake parcels for students to take with them. She looked over at me and we both grinned in excitement. Everything was going really well. Almost every stall on the ground was occupied by students.

After the first group left, another stopped by, and then another. Soon, my Chai became popular among people. At some point, there was a queue of 9, waiting for me to serve Chai. I was so happy, I kept extra tea ready all the time.

Rutu's Scrunchies and scarves became bestsellers. "Glad I brought loads," she beamed, opening more packets of scrunchies.

We helped each other whenever we could. It was getting overwhelming, but we were enjoying it. As lunchtime approached, we saw more local newspapers and journalists arriving at the event. They got down from the cars holding cameras and notepads, ready to capture everything.

I quickly prepared more food and whisked eggs so I could make Omelettes fasters. Sandwiches partially assembled, I brewed more chai and coffee.

Soon enough, all the local journalists scattered around to talk to students, professors, and stall owners. I braced myself as two men and a woman walked towards my stall.

"Among The Pages Book Café. Interesting." A tall man in his late thirties smiled at me. "How's everything going?"

"Fantastic," I beamed. The second man was recording and it made me anxious. But I wanted to make the most out of it. "What would you like to have?"

"Oh, Chai please, and are those samosas?" he pointed at the tray of mini samosas. "Looks nice. I'll have that as well."

I served three cups of tea and plated samosas while answering their questions. They asked where to find my café and what's the specialty of my café. "My book café, it's a book house actually, has a great collection of books. And as you enjoy the meals in the garden, my beautiful four dogs will keep you a friendly company." They chuckled and asked some more questions. I told them about Rhythm Lane and handed them the café's pamphlet. They asked how did I find out about the event and what are my thoughts about it. "A friend of mine is a student here. She informed me and my friends about the event." When I told them Rutu, Nupur, and I are best friends, the female journalist said, "We should do your interview together. It will give our young female readers motivation to start their businesses."

Happy with her idea, we agreed and answered every question carefully, making sure anyone who reads it will give their dreams a chance.

"Rhythm Lane, did you say?" the man asked again. "We will visit soon."

"Anytime. I'm sure you'll like it there," I replied.

When our interview was done, we hardly had any time to scream in excitement. More students and professors stopped by our stalls. Some of them bought books. So far, I could sell 20 out of 50 books, which was decent. Double Egg Rolls, Omelettes, and Paneer Rolls were most in-demand during lunchtime. I made sure to prepare rolls with extra stuffing and sauce.

It was almost mid-afternoon when Vihaan came back to join us. I was both happy and relieved to see him.

"How's everything?" he asked as he joined my stall.

"It's amazing, Vihaan. You should see what these students are presenting on the stage. You would love it."

He chuckled. "Okay."

Rutu peeked at me from her stall and said, "Avni. I'm really very hungry."

"Me too," Nupur announced from her stall.

"What would you like to eat?" I asked as I turned on my induction. My best friends demanded Cheesy Omelettes and Spicy Paneer Rolls with Cold Coffee on the side. As I prepared our lunch, girls dragged their chairs next to my stall and sat down with Vihaan to catch up on our much-needed break.

"So Vihaan," I heard Rutu say. "How serious are you about our best friend? You love her?"

I laughed as I flipped the Roll on the pan. Last night, I told them about Vihaan and their reaction was exactly how I expected, loud and not at all subtle. They didn't get a proper chance to tease us and this was their opportunity.

"If you hurt her, you know we will not leave you alone?" Nupur joined in.

He laughed, "No I won't hurt her and yes, I am very serious about her. You have nothing to worry about, but you are free to ask me any questions."

"Fine," Nupur said. "Since you are like my brother, I trust you. But you have to take us all to dinner. Promise?"

"Okay," he said. Turning towards me with a small smile on his face.

I knew my friends won't leave us alone. But I like how both of them care about me. I let them tease him because he was really good with answers. It was fun to watch them get along. We ate lunch and slurped cold coffee until our break was over.

As the presentations on the stage resumed, we all got back to work too. With our tummies full, we girls started working with more enthusiasm. Vihaan decided to roam around to meet students and new people to network with them.

Prachiti brought her friends to meet us. Some of her reader friends purchased books from me and took my pamphlets to visit my book café soon. They all purchased something from all three of us and clicked selfies with us.

"Tomorrow, newspapers will have a story of this event. All the stall names would be mentioned too. And whoever took your interview, they'll post it on social media," Prachiti told us.

I pulled her into a hug and promised that we will give her a party soon, for we were really grateful to participate in the event because of her. She smiled and stayed with us until the end of the event.

All the presentations were done before 7 in the evening. Even after that, students stopped by to parcel food and celebrate with pastries. Even boys purchased Rutu's fashion accessories for their sisters and girlfriends. As the day slowed down around us, we packed up our stalls. We all ended up making a pretty decent profit, our money bags full of happiness.

Before leaving, Nupur, Rutu, and I decided to say *Hi* to all the other stall owners and followed each other on social media to stay in touch. It was a pretty good event for all of us.

Vihaan helped us load everything in the van and pulled the van out of the parking lot.

"Let's go eat some ice cream," I suggested as we drove out of the college.

Before my friends could reply, Nupur's phone rang.

"It's Tanvi Vahini," she told me, answering the call.

"What?" I checked my phone. It was on silent, I missed 20 missed calls from her and Aai.

"Yeah, hold on," Nupur said to Vahini and handed her phone to me.

"Vahini? What is it?"

Her voice came shaky and panicked, "Avni. Come to the café soon. Madhav Kaka is here and..."

"What? No Vahini wait," my throat dried and I could hardly get the words out. "Is Vidya kaki with him?"

"No," she said. I could feel she was scared. "Come soon okay?"

"I'm on my way Vahini. Just don't do anything until I return. Don't let Aai do anything."

I hung up the call. Fear went humming down my body. When he said he'll visit soon, I didn't know this soon. I thought I had it all figured out. But now, I'm not so sure. I had to be there, with my family. I had to stop it all.

"Avni?" I heard my name around me. All three faces were scanning mine with concern. "What happened?" Nupur asked.

"Drive faster. We need to get to the cafe," I managed to tell Vihaan.

TWENTY

My Baba used to say, "When you think there's even a small chance, a tiny possibility of getting something you want; you must hold on to that chance, grab it, pull it towards you, and make it yours." That's what I planned to do, no matter how terrified I felt.

When we reached Rhythm Lane, I saw Aai, Vahini, and Chaturvedi Ajji-Ajoba seated in the cafe. Madhav Kaka was talking to Aai, who looked miserable but calm.

"Aai?" I entered the café, closely accompanied by my friends. "What's going on?"

Vahini pulled me aside and whispered, "Why didn't you tell us he messaged you about the documents and the partial amount?"

Before I could reply, Madhav Kaka interrupted. "Now that she's here, we can get it over with."

I turned to face him. He was trying to appear confident but I could see impatience in his eyes. He was rubbing his hand on his left knee, waiting for me to say something.

Vahini started panicking next to me. I held her hand and looked her in the eyes, "I've got this, okay?"

She didn't know what I meant by that, but she nodded and stayed by my side. I sat next to my mother and greeted Madhav Kaka with a smile. "Glad you are here, Madhav Kaka. You are right, we can get it over with."

Aai and Vahini looked at me with confusion. Even Kaka's expressions slightly shifted. Concern took over the earlier confidence, but he managed not to give in.

I fished out Baba's passbook that I had kept in my bag just in case. Opening the page of the transaction between Madhav Kaka and Baba, I showed the passbook to everyone.

"This here," I pointed at the highlighted transaction, "is the money you are asking now. Looks like my Baba already paid you. We don't owe you anything, Kaka. And I believe, you don't own anything in this store anymore."

Aai and Vahini were glancing between me and Kaka with astonishment. I could sense their nervousness. Aai leaned towards me and whispered, "Avu? When did you find it out?"

"I'll explain later Aai. You have nothing to worry about," I assured her. She has tolerated enough stress in her life. She doesn't deserve this.

"This is an old transaction," Madhav Kaka attempted to explain it. "And it was not about the..."

"Come on, Kaka. The transaction entry is pretty clear. Why are you doing this?"

As he was about to say something unreasonable, Vidya Kaki entered the café, holding a file. That's what I had been waiting for. When I suspected that the real documents might be in Madhav Kaka's possession, I had to call her to help me. When I told her what her husband was up to, she was furious at him.

"I'll see what I can do, Avni Beti. Don't you worry," she said to me on a call yesterday. Troubling her wasn't in my mind. But she was my last hope and I had to take that chance.

"Vidya!" Kaka fumed at her. His eyes widened in anger. "What are you doing here?"

"Cleaning up your mess," she spat back, giving him a disgusted look. She took a seat next to me, away from her husband's reach, and handed me the file.

I drew a deep breath and pulled out papers from the file, anxiously hoping those were the correct documents. And I was right. The transaction was done. All the paperwork was done. Madhav Kaka didn't have anything to do with the store anymore.

"Where did you find it?" Madhav Kaka looked horrified. He glared at Vidya kaki so furiously, anyone would have been scared. But Vidya kaki held back his glare with one of her own.

"I'm ashamed of you, Madhav." She shook her head. "I can't believe you did this to your own family."

"You didn't even know about this. Then how did you find those documents?" He asked impatiently.

"Avni suspected it," Vidya kaki replied. "How did you assume she wouldn't figure out a way?"

Kaka fell silent.

Aai, who was still trying to process everything, asked him, "Why Bhau? Why did you do it?"

Kaka had nothing to say. As he remained silent, Vidya Kaki answered Aai's question. "He lost his job 2 years ago, Amrita. And recently, he's been doing shady things. I don't dare ask. But money has been a problem for a long time. He tried to borrow money from friends. Some of them knock on my door to ask for their money back. I don't have anything. And Madhav? He doesn't care. Even now he must have done something stupid and needs money."

She held Aai's hand and continued, "If I knew about his intentions earlier, I would have stopped him, Amrita. I'm sorry."

Aai nodded and dabbed her eyes with her saree. She reached for my and Vahini's hand to hold. Both Vahini and I shifted closer to her, making sure she was okay. It was too much to take. Our own family member troubled us, and for what? Just some money. He could have asked for it.

"Kaka," I softly broke the silence. My heart pounded with anger. But I'm Baba's daughter and he taught me well. "If you still...if you need money, we can help you. If there's any problem you can tell us. Just don't try to trick anyone. It's not worth it Kaka. You know better than that."

I felt confident and light when I said it. He stared down and refused to meet my gaze. But when I said, "Baba trusted you Kaka. I hope you know that," he looked straight into my eyes. A flicker of shame flashed on his face, still, he didn't say a word.

Vidya Kaki's eyes teared up. She glanced at me and said, "I'm sorry, Avni."

"No Kaki," I held her hand. "It's not your fault. Thank you for helping me."

"Thank you, Vidya," Aai whispered.

She looked tired but relieved as it was over. I wrapped my arm around her shoulder and said, "It's done Aai. Nothing to worry about now."

For a while, nobody said anything. Nothing was left to be said. Quietness filled the room until Chaturvedi Ajoba cleared his throat and politely said, "Madhav, I wasn't aware of any of this. But you must know that Arun was like my son. This is my family. And next time if you ever try to do something like this, I'll be here."

Madhav Kaka closed his eyes and sighed defencelessly. He cupped his knees and got up from his seat. With one last look at all of us, he walked towards the door to leave. He waited at the doorway for Vidya Kaki. And when she didn't join him, he just walked out of the café, without saying a word. I wasn't expecting any response from him but I'm sure he won't do any of this ever again.

Tanvi Vahini, who was sitting quietly for a long time, asked Vidya Kaki, "Kaki, Is there anything we could help you with?"

Vidya Kaki gently caressed Vahini's head and replied, "No dear. Madhav will come around, don't worry. He is not a bad man, he just forgot to be a good man."

"Stay with us for a few days," I offered. "Let him be on his own for a while."

She laughed, "I wouldn't say no to such a generous offer. But..."

"Please Vidya," Aai added softly. "It's been years. Stay with us. We have so much to talk about."

Vidya Kaki smiled, "Sure. I'd like that."

I was glad that it all worked out. It didn't have to happen like this though. There's always an easy way to deal with anything, but for some reason, people often prefer not to see it. If only Kaka had talked to us about his problems and this whole thing could have been avoided.

It doesn't matter now. All that matters is- Among The Pages belongs to us. Only us.

Baba, if you are listening, thank you for making sure we were okay even after you left. Thank you for everything that you did for me. I wish I could hug you.

After Madhav Kaka left, Vahini brewed some chai for everyone. As we were talking, Mahima Kaki and Sudhir Kaka brought Nidhi and my pets into the café.

"Attu!" Nidhi freed herself from Mahima Kaki's hand and ran into my arms. "Where were you all day?"

I pulled her closer. "I was at the big event. I will tell you all about it later."

My pets ran to greet me too. I kissed them all and let them circle me with joy.

I glanced around myself. My entire family was with me, in *our* book café. I don't think I felt this happier in a long while. This is all I wanted, my family smiling.

When Aai, Kaki, and Vahini went home, Nidhi and my pets stayed with me. I thanked Chaturvedi Ajji and Ajoba for staying with Aai. Rutu and Nupur hugged me and then scolded me for not telling them what was happening with the cafe.

When everyone left, Vihaan stayed to help me close the café. "You were very brave," he whispered. "And I'm so proud of you."

I smiled and hugged him quickly when Nidhi wasn't looking. He chuckled and said, "Let's go."

I locked *my* book café, looking forward to opening it with nothing to worry about. As we all began walking, Nidhi demanded that Vihaan carry her on his back. "My legs hurt," she told him. He happily scooped her up on his back.

With my beloved pets, my beautiful niece smiling wide, and Vihaan by my side, I walked home.

TWENTY-ONE

EPILOGUE: DIWALI

Vihaan

My whole life, I've been living in houses that never belonged to me. It was always an employee quarter assigned to Baba. Aai never got a chance to decorate it the way a home should be. But we all got used to it. Even now, both of them are in Delhi for their jobs, celebrating Diwali on a video call with us. They're happy for me, but they were hoping I would join them for Diwali. Ajji said she would never talk to me if I left. Not that I was planning to go, because this Diwali is special for me.

Ajji is cooking everything that I love. The aroma of Laddus, Chakli, Chiwda, and all kinds of snacks is a new normal these days. Every day, I wake up to find Ajji cooking something new. If I keep eating like this, soon my tummy will be out. But it'll be worth it.

Last week, Avni and I went shopping. We purchased a lot of things for Diwali decorations and gifts for everyone. She bought me a new Kurta and I got her a Paithani Saree. When she saw that saree in the shop, her eyes sparkled. And when I said let's buy it, she hugged me in the middle of the shopping mall. As I wore the Kurta she gifted me for the evening celebration, I couldn't wait to see her in a saree.

At 6 in the evening, Ajoba, Ajji, and I went downstairs to do *Lakshmipoojan* at our dairy. This year, Ajoba let me do the pooja. Ajji was giving me instructions as I presented the *Naividya* offerings to the goddess of wealth and prosperity. Ajoba winked at me, indicating I should steal the sweets as soon as Ajji looks away.

When we were done with our Pooja, we made our way to Among The Pages. Avni and Tanvi Vahini had drawn a beautiful *Rangoli* design in front of the door, sprinkled with flower petals and complimented with *Diyas*.

The doorframe of the book cafe was decorated with flower garlands, diyas were outlining the front wall, and fairy lights were twinkling everywhere. We entered the cafe to find Nupur and her parents, Rutu, Doctor Kaka, neighborhood families, Avni's Aai, and her Vahini seated with Diwali snacks kept on the table between them. Tanvi Vahini's parents also decided to celebrate Diwali at Rhythm Lane. I'm sure they'll love it here.

"Vihaan, come join us," Avni's mother said to me, greeting my grandparents by touching their feet. I did the same and touched her feet to take blessing.

"Happy Diwali, Kaki," I smiled at her.

"Happy Diwali, Son," she cheerfully replied.

Little Nidhi ran towards me and jumped so I could catch her in my arms. I picked her up and pulled her cheeks. She told me about her Diwali adventures and I listened wondering how can she talk so much. Then I remembered, she is Avni's niece, can't expect less.

Putting her back down on the floor, I watched as she ran towards the pets. Today, even they were wearing new dresses, all groomed up. Cookie's hairbow was a topic of discussion.

I sat between my new family and looked around to search for Avni.

"She's in the kitchen," Tanvi Vahini whispered. "Making Laddus. You can go if you want."

"Really?" I asked. Because that's what I wanted to do.

"Of course not," she giggled. "Wait here. She'll be out any minute."

I kept my gaze hooked on the kitchen door, so I won't miss the entrance of Chef Avni Joshi. And soon enough, she walked out of the kitchen holding a tray full of Laddus. She looked ten times more gorgeous in her saree. Her long curly hair was bouncing and anklets were tinkling as she walked. When she smiled at me, my heart went wild. Her nosering, the zumkas from Tulshibaug, her new bangles, the delicate necklace, everything looked so perfect.

Vahini and Nupur cleared their throats, but I didn't care. I wanted to look at my beautiful girlfriend. She is glowing every day as her book cafe is blooming.

Even though Madhav kaka troubled them, Avni and her family are trying to help him. He eventually apologized and is trying his best to make things right. Vidya Kaki visits at least once a month to meet us. It's all good.

Now Avni is doing everything she wanted to do for the book cafe. The website is bringing decent traffic, with more than 20 book box subscriptions each month. At least 4 more people and groups signed up for Work-From-Café and three writers booked a nook. As planned, Prachiti is conducting a monthly book club with Avni and 6 other girls who can talk about books for hours.

The event in Prachiti's college turned out to be amazing for Avni, Nupur, and Rutu. Their interview was posted on social media and published on the news website. The news article praised each stall at the event. Soon, Among The

Pages' social media followers started growing consistently. Her book cafe is busy every day, Avni hardly has time for herself. She might need to hire an assistant chef now.

And me? I'm still doing the same job, but my App is progressing. Nishant is helping me with the marketing. It'll be ready for the final trial in a couple of months. I have so many ideas to turn it into a proper business and I'm sure it'll happen sooner or later. All in all, I am happy in Pune.

Avni kept the plate of Laddus on the table and served it to everyone. People around us were busy talking, laughing, complimenting each other's new dresses, and eating Diwali sweets.

I bit into the Laddu and it was so delicious, the sweetness exploded in my mouth.

"I'm learning." Avni bit her tongue.

"It's perfect," I smiled at her. "Happy Diwali."

"Happy Diwali handsome," she whispered.

"Laddus are delicious, Avni." Everybody praised her as she served more.

As the Diwali night uncurled, we all played *Antakshari*. Nidhi was dancing here and there, brightening up the celebration. I video-called my parents to involve them in Rhythm Lane's Diwali. Since the day they talked to Avni on a video call, they call her more than they call me. And now they are eager to meet everyone. "We'll visit soon," Aai said to Ajji the other day.

Later that evening, when everyone went home, I brought Ajoba's minivan out of the parking lot as Avni locked her book café.

"Ready to go?"

"Absolutely," she beamed. Her rosy pink lips curved up into a smile as she hopped into the passenger's seat.

Shifting the gear, I pulled the van onto the road.

"Did you like Rhythm Lane Diwali?" she asked, playing with her hair strand.

"I loved it," I replied. "Aai and Baba loved it too, even though virtually."

"Do you miss them?"

"Yes," I confessed. "But I understand Baba's job. He is a busy man. Nowadays, he keeps saying he will take early retirement and we will get a new house here on Rhythm Lane."

"That's so nice," she replied. "I can't wait to meet them in person."

"They are excited to meet you too."

I drove for another 10 minutes to reach our destination. People were celebrating Diwali everywhere I looked. Shops and houses were decorated and little kids had built beautiful mud castles in front of their houses. I felt glad that I decided to celebrate Diwali with Ajji-Ajoba, and Avni.

"It still looks the same," I said as we got down from the van.

"I know right?" She held my hand and smiled. "Harsh Dada used to bring me here quite often."

"Especially when you cried?"

She chuckled, "Yeah. Which was quite often."

"What would you like to have?" I asked, wrapping my arm around her shoulder.

"Choco Chip Chocolate ice cream," she replied almost instantly. "And you?"

"I'll take Mango."

I placed the order and stood next to Avni, watching the vibrantly glowing city around us.

When our ice cream was ready, instead of going back into the minivan, we stood on the sidewalk watching people and vehicles pass by. Enjoying ice cream in the middle of winter was very unlikely for me. But Avni doesn't believe in such things. She says, if you feel like eating it, you eat it. Simple! What's worst could happen? You'll fall sick for a day, but you'll be happy.

I looked at my gorgeous girlfriend and found her already glancing at me.

"What?" I asked.

"Nothing," she smiled softly. "Just happy to be here with you."

"Me too."

We walked towards the van and leaned against the hood to watch the city celebrating the festival of lights. Beautiful firecrackers flashed into the sky above us. Avni hooked her hand into my arm and rested her head on my shoulder.

When I planted a soft kiss on her forehead, she looked at me and smiled. At that moment, I decided to be the reason behind her smile for the rest of my life.

About The Author

Rucha Pantoji is the author of "What Does Your Dad Do?" a memoir she wrote for her father.

She started writing stories when she was in school, hoping one day she would publish her book. But as she grew up, destiny brought her into an Engineering College and she briefly pretended to have her life together by taking a (pretty boring) tech job.

After hating her job and complaining about it every damn day, she finally decided to write stories rather than lines of codes.

Now she spends her day writing stories and night curled up in a bed with a book until her eyes burn. Brewing a refreshing Chai is her hobby apart from collecting cute stationery and handbags.

Find Out More About Rucha: https://www.ruchapantoji.com/

~

Enjoyed visiting Among The Pages Book Café? Support my Indie Author Journey by leaving a rating and review on Amazon and Goodreads. It would mean the world to me.

Subscribe to my Newsletter (https://www.ruchapantoji.com/) to receive updates about Rhythm Lane and more stories.

Say Hi to me on Social Media.

· Instagram- @ruchapantoji
· Facebook- @authorruchapantoji
· Goodreads- Rucha Pantoji

Note From The Author

Dear Reader,

Thanks a lot for reading 'Dreaming Among The Pages'. If any of the incidents put a smile on your face, I'd be beyond happy.

I always like to connect with readers and fellow writers. Feel free to contact me if you have anything to share with me. I would love to know what you are working on.

I tried my best to avoid typos. However, sometimes, mistakes do slip through unintentionally. If you found any mistakes, please email me at hello@ruchapantoji.com or message me on Instagram.

Once again, thank you for reading my book :)